This item must be returned or renewed on or before the latest date shown

23 AUG

KT-147-959

CIRCUS ACT

Spy Dog and Spy Pups are works of fiction. Andrew Cope wants to make it absolutely clear that the dogs are not based on any animal, living or dead, because that would just be silly*.

* Small print . . . OK, admittedly Andrew does have a pet dog called Lara. And she's black and white, a bit like the one in the Spy Dog books. And the dog in the books is also called Lara. But that could just be a coincidence. And the sticky-up ear is just a random coincidence too. Apart from those similarities, the books have no connection with the dog at all. Andrew also has a puppy called LJ. And the dogs in this story are called Spud and Star so that settles it. Even the names are different. So there! And another thing, the dogs in the book are dead clever. And Andrew's dogs are really stupid. They have no talent whatsoever. This is how daft they are: if he tells them to sit, they lie down. And if he tells them to lie down, they shake a paw! Duh! And they haven't got mobile phones or gadgets. None of his dogs can drive a car or send emails. They don't go on adventures and have never actually caught a baddie (although Lara did nip the postman once, but I don't think he's a baddie). And the dogs absolutely cannot beat Andrew at computer games. Ever! Got it? So, please don't keep asking if the Spy Dog or Spy Pups books are based on his actual dogs. I mean, if you wrote a book called *Spy Guinea Pig*, wouldn't you get sick of people coming up to you and saying, 'Hey dude, is this story based on your real guinea pig?' Cos you'd roll your eyes and go, 'As if. My guinea pig isn't a spy. He's actually an evil baddie called Jeremy who wears small leather gloves on his tiny piggy hands and he cackles with an evil laugh and is going to destroy the world.' And your mates would go 'No way,' and you'd go 'Yes way,' and you'd probably go and write a story about it. But that wouldn't make it real. Just like J. K. Rowling and Harry Potter. That's not real (J. K. is but Harry isn't). It's just a story. In the same way that Spy Pups *Circus Act* is ju... a relief. I just tho.. y bothered to read .... ase get on with th.......

X62 660 29X

0 030 830 08X

If you want Lara or her puppy to visit your school, please email her at lara@artofbrilliance.co.uk. They'll probably have to bring Andrew Cope along too, but don't let that put you off. Or you can find out more about the Spy Dog and Spy Pups books online at *www.spydog451.co.uk*, where there are pictures, videos and competitions too!

Books by Andrew Cope

Spy Dog
Spy Dog 2
Spy Dog Unleashed!
Spy Dog Superbrain
Spy Dog Rocket Rider

Spy Pups Treasure Quest
Spy Pups Prison Break
Spy Pups Circus Act

SPY PUPS
CIRCUS ACT

SEFTON LIBRARY SERVICES	
002709929	
Bertrams	11/08/2010
Jhc	
MDW	£4.99

PUFFIN BOOKS

Published by the Penguin Group
Penguin Books Ltd, 80 Strand, London WC2R ORL, England
Penguin Group (USA) Inc., 375 Hudson Street, New York, New York 10014, USA
Penguin Group (Canada), 90 Eglinton Avenue East, Suite 700, Toronto, Ontario, Canada M4P 2Y3
(a division of Pearson Penguin Canada Inc.)
Penguin Ireland, 25 St Stephen's Green, Dublin 2, Ireland (a division of Penguin Books Ltd)
Penguin Group (Australia), 250 Camberwell Road, Camberwell, Victoria 3124, Australia
(a division of Pearson Australia Group Pty Ltd)
Penguin Books India Pvt Ltd, 11 Community Centre, Panchsheel Park, New Delhi – 110 017, India
Penguin Group (NZ), 67 Apollo Drive, Rosedale, North Shore 0632, New Zealand
(a division of Pearson New Zealand Ltd)
Penguin Books (South Africa) (Pty) Ltd, 24 Sturdee Avenue, Rosebank,
Johannesburg 2196, South Africa

Penguin Books Ltd, Registered Offices: 80 Strand, London WC2R ORL, England

puffinbooks.com

First published 2010
1

Text copyright © Andrew Cope, 2010
Illustrations copyright © James de la Rue, 2010
All rights reserved

The moral right of the author and illustrator has been asserted

Set in Bembo 15/18 pt
Typeset by Palimpsest Book Production Limited, Falkirk, Stirlingshire
Made and printed in England by Clays Ltd, St Ives plc

Except in the United States of America, this book is sold subject to the condition
that it shall not, by way of trade or otherwise, be lent, re-sold, hired out, or otherwise
circulated without the publisher's prior consent in any form of binding or cover other
than that in which it is published and without a similar condition including this condition
being imposed on the subsequent purchaser

British Library Cataloguing in Publication Data
A CIP catalogue record for this book is available from the British Library

ISBN: 978-0-141-32605-4

www.greenpenguin.co.uk

Mixed Sources
Product group from well-managed
forests and other controlled sources
www.fsc.org Cert no. SA-COC-1592
© 1996 Forest Stewardship Council

Penguin Books is committed to a sustainable future
for our business, our readers and our planet.
The book in your hands is made from paper
certified by the Forest Stewardship Council.

For my favourite children

Thanks to:

The Puffin clan. Especially Shannon who's
got the best job title ever!

James de la Rue for such cool pics . . . again!

Max Lowson for a million and one ideas
(shame I have to sit through a million
rubbish ones before I get to the one!).

French Tony for the good humour and
world-class eyebrows!

Ollie for test marketing the manuscript.

Louise for ideas, patience and
encouragement.

Contents

1. Feeding Time

The castle drawbridge was lowered and the car swept into the courtyard. The driver checked himself in the rear-view mirror. He smoothed his eyebrows the best he could and took a deep breath to compose himself. Beside him on the passenger seat was a very important briefcase.

He parked in front of the castle then stepped out of the car and handcuffed the briefcase to his wrist. Then he approached the castle's huge door and pulled the bell cord. He straightened his tie as he waited.

The door opened and a butler let him into the reception room. No words were necessary. He was led through the drawing room and past portraits and suits of armour. Their footsteps echoed up a winding stone staircase before the men entered a modern white room where a lady was waiting. She cradled a fluffy white cat in her left arm, stroking it with her right hand. The diamond on the cat's collar gleamed in the sunlight.

The man approached the desk, unlocked the handcuff and put the briefcase on the glass table. A bulky security guard moved to stand by the door and block the exit. The man sat nervously, his eyes darting around the room, which looked completely different to the rest of the castle. But the views were spectacular – rolling hills, brooding moors; they were miles from anywhere. A huge fish tank took up the whole of the left-hand wall, where hundreds of fish darted through the water.

'Greetings, Tony,' said the lady, who was also in white, almost invisible against the walls. She stopped stroking the cat and flicked open the briefcase. The gems inside sparkled, but the lady looked disappointed. 'The deal was supposed to be worth one million,' she said without emotion.

'I know, mistress, and I'm sorry. It's just that, well, times are hard. Business is difficult. The police have been watching us.'

The lady nodded knowingly. 'But the deal was one million,' she reminded him. 'You

promised. What am I supposed to think, Tony? That your promises are worthless?'

The man looked at the floor. 'I need more time,' he said. 'One more week. We've got a new venue and a new opportunity. It should be a big one.'

The lady nodded to the security guard. 'Feed the fish,' she ordered. The muscle man walked to the glass tank. He reached into a bucket, pulled out two raw steaks and threw them into the aquarium. There was a frenzy of action as the fish tore the meat apart. The lady smiled. The cat purred. The man's face twitched. Mealtime took less than thirty seconds and the tank returned to its tranquil state.

'Piranhas!' said the man, sweat breaking out on his top lip.

'Piranhas, indeed,' said the lady in white. 'And they're still peckish.'

The man gulped. 'Like I said, one more week.'

The lady smiled a watery smile and her cat purred louder. 'Imagine how hungry my fish will be in one week, Tony,' she said. 'Please don't let me down.'

2. Grand Master

Professor Cortex mopped his brow. His eyes never left the chessboard as he stuffed his hanky back into his top pocket. He sighed. And nodded knowingly. This was quite a game. He glanced at his opponent and was irritated by her calm exterior.

She's good, he thought, *but she's only a novice.*

The scientist took hold of the queen and slid her on to a new square. He kept his fingers on the chess piece while he ran through his opponent's next probable move in his head. Once he was confident that his was the right decision, he removed his fingers and looked up. 'Ha,' he coughed. 'What do you make of that?'

His challenger nodded knowingly. This was a big moment. She knew that the professor had never lost a chess match in his life. He'd beaten

grand masters from all over the world. He'd even programmed computer chess games and was acknowledged as one of the country's top chess players. Yet here he was, about to be beaten by a dog.

Lara took her time. This was a moment to savour. Her puppies wagged enthusiastically.

'What now, Ma?' whined Spud, his big eyes peering up at her. 'Has he got you?'

Lara smiled a doggie smile. *Certainly not! I've got him.* She twitched her whiskers and adjusted her spectacles so they were on the end of her long nose. Then she reached a paw towards her queen. Carefully and very precisely she slid the piece across the board and knocked over the opposing piece. Lara's bullet-holed ear stood proud. *Game over, I believe?* she thought. *Victory for the canine species! Checkmate!*

The professor had gone white. 'But . . .' he began. 'How?' he spluttered. 'I mean, where did *that* move come from? This is chess. I never lose at chess.'

Well, you just have, Prof, smiled Lara. *You've just been outfoxed by a mutt.*

'Have you won, Ma?' woofed Star, her tail on wag-factor ten. With her black and white splodges she looked just like a mini version of her mum. They even had the same sticky-up ear.

'She has,' yelped Spud, who had the same black coat as his pedigree father. 'The prof's lost his first ever game! You're a genius dog, Ma.'

'Not genius dog,' corrected Lara. 'I'm a Spy Dog.' She raised an eyebrow and looked at her puppies. 'Retired!' Lara stood and offered the professor a paw. He shook graciously. The bewildered old man sank into his comfortable armchair and Lara helped herself to a glass of lime and lemonade. *Shaken, not stirred*, she thought.

Lara reflected on the last two years. *It's been such a brilliant time*, she thought. *My career as a spy dog was very exciting. But family life is bliss. Who'd have thought, when I adopted the Cooks, that I'd settle in so quickly. Or so brilliantly!* Lara looked at her mentor, Professor Maximus Cortex. *I owe him so much*, she thought. *His accelerated learning programme and home-made brain formula has made me into a super-intelligent canine. And now my puppies are taking it all on board.* She gave the professor a huge lemon and lime lick. *Don't worry, old fella*, she wagged. *Beginner's luck! Why don't we play Monopoly? You always beat me at that.*

Lara slurped on her drink and glanced at her puppies. Star had turned her attention to a crossword puzzle, filling in the spaces with a pencil held expertly in her mouth. Her brother was lounging on a beanbag, loading a computer game. Lara looked at his rolls of fat and considered whether she should cut out his afternoon snack. *It's just puppy fat*, she decided. *He's got a lot more growing to do yet.*

Spud and Star were incredibly proud of their mum. Lara was the world's first ever spy dog

– and their mission was to follow in her paw prints. The puppies were nearly five months old now and desperate for some secret-agent action. Lara wasn't so keen. She'd given up being 'Agent GM451' and was focused on being the best mum she could be. *And that means keeping my pups and the Cook family safe.*

The spy dog sat back in her chair and closed her eyes. *This feels great*, she thought. *Being a mum is the best thing ever. Family bliss. Oodles of love. Peace and quiet. No more action and adventure for me!*

Lara had no idea how wrong she could be.

3. K9XLR8R

Today the dogs had made their monthly visit to Professor Cortex's Spy School. Although she was retired, Lara thought it was important to keep up to date with new developments. She loved the professor and knew Spud and Star were excited about being spy pups, but she wanted to protect them from danger. *I'll play along*, she decided. After all, Lara knew she could never escape from her spy dog past. Enemy agents could still be stalking her, so it paid for them all to be up to speed with the latest the professor had to offer. *Better safe than sorry!*

The old man hadn't spoken for an hour. He seemed very deflated by his chess defeat. Star made him a cup of Earl Grey tea. She put it on a tray and carefully walked into the office to present him with his drink. The professor took the cup. 'Defeated by a dog,' he said, staring into space.

But not any old dog, wagged Star. *She's the cleverest, coolest dog on the planet. And she's my mum! She's caught dozens of baddies and outwitted some very clever crims. So don't feel bad, old fella. She's the best of the best.*

Just then the door opened and the Cook family burst in. The children tumbled through the door, a trio of enthusiastic smiles. Sophie ran to Star and cuddled her so tightly that her eyes bulged. *Steady girl*, Star thought, struggling to loosen herself from the iron grip of affection.

Ollie had made a beeline for Spud. The pup sat and shook paws with the youngest child. They were good mates and could often be found playing computer games together. Ollie and Spud had a homework pact. Spud helped Ollie out with his numeracy and, in return, Ollie would do an hour of wrestling practice to hone the dog's skills.

Ben was the eldest. He made straight for his beloved Lara. The pups were cute, but Lara was his. The Cook family had visited the RSPCA on Ben's tenth birthday with the aim of adopting a pet. Little did they know that it was

Lara who chose them! But the children soon realized she was an extraordinary dog.

'Sitting on the toilet doing a poo is hardly normal doggie behaviour,' Ben explained to his brother and sister. The children had kept Lara's special abilities secret for as long as they could, but a daring car chase through the village had got everything out into the open. *A driving dog is a dead giveaway*, Ben had thought to himself.

'How's your day been, girl?' he asked, stroking his pet's head.

Oh, you know, shrugged Lara. *Karate lessons, helicopter simulator, weapons training and generally hanging out with the prof. Beat him at chess . . . that kind of thing.*

Ollie noticed Professor Cortex sitting quietly in a chair. 'How have they been?' he asked.

'Extraordinary,' muttered the professor, staring into space, still in shock after his loss.

Spud and Star almost wagged their tails off. 'Hear that, sis?' woofed Spud. 'We're extraordinary!'

The puppies were certainly special. Their mum's genes had been passed down and they were very quick learners. But they'd also had a helping hand. Both dogs had spent most of

the day in the learning lab, wired up to the professor's brand-new 'Fastbrain K9XLR8R'. This accelerated-learning machine meant they could understand several languages, including English, Chinese, basic cat and horse. Star was ultra-clever. She'd even mastered Siamese cat, the hardest feline dialect of them all.

Spud was more of an adventurer. While his sister was happy to absorb herself in lessons, he wanted to get active. He was always sniffing for action. He was best at practical stuff like sending emails, martial arts and map reading. Star's brains and Spud's practical skills made them a formidable team. They'd already had a couple of accidental adventures and were longing for the day when a real spy mission came their way. Unfortunately, their mum didn't seem quite so keen.

Mr and Mrs Cook wandered into the staffroom. Dad loosened his tie after a long day at work. 'Good evening, Professor,' he said. 'What's lined up for us tonight?'

The professor struggled out of his armchair and took a deep breath to clear his head. 'Well,' he began, 'I've had GM451 and her pups all day. Been putting them through their paces. Intelligence is excellent. Fitness levels are generally good, although this little fella could do with fewer calories per day.'

Spud's tail drooped. *But calories are my favourite thing.*

'But I've saved the gadgets and really interesting stuff for this evening. I know the kids like my inventions,' he smiled, nodding to Ollie, Sophie and Ben. Ollie was beaming. Sophie's eyes shone and Ben high-fived his sister in excitement. The professor's inventions were sometimes completely mad and impractical, but always interesting. They even had some at home. Ollie was always using his poocam to spy on next door. And George, the neighbourhood-watch tortoise, was getting very good with his rocket-propelled skateboard. Last week there had been a dramatic rescue when he'd skidded into the canal, but apart from that mishap, he was breaking tortoise land-speed records every day.

'So what have you got for us, Prof?' asked Dad, hopping about, as excited as his children. Mum just smiled and rolled her eyes. She was a bit more suspicious of the professor's inventions and all the trouble he seemed to get the children involved in 'accidentally'. She was waiting for the day he invented something useful, like an automatic bedroom-tidier.

'Plenty,' beamed the professor, rubbing his hands together like a fly. 'In fact, I've got some of the best gadgets ever this month,' he said. 'Follow me to the inventing room.'

4. Gadgets Galore

'Righty-ho,' began Professor Cortex. 'Remember, it's not all about spying. Government cutbacks mean that I'm having to invent everyday items — anything that we can patent that will earn us some money. That's how my research is funded. Follow me,' he said, finally regaining his enthusiasm.

Everyone trotted behind the professor as he marched along a corridor to a door marked Inventions Room.

'Top secret, obviously,' he reminded them as he pressed his hand against the security pad and his fingerprints were confirmed.

The door

swished open and the group entered a little nervously. 'Let's start with this,' said the professor, picking up a blue helmet. 'Something revolutionary. It's still experimental, but this one may change the way we live forever!' He looked at Mr Cook and frowned. 'Your hair, sir, could do with a trim.'

'Yes,' agreed Dad, running his fingers through his thick hair. 'I just haven't had time.'

'Well, luckily for you, I have the perfect solution for busy people such as yourself,' nodded the professor, tapping the helmet. 'This is an automatic hair trimmer. I call it the "Haircut 100".' He held it out. 'Fancy a go?'

Dad shied away. 'I don't think so, Professor,' he said. 'I'd prefer to go to the barber's.'

Mrs Cook nodded in agreement. She remembered the time the professor claimed to have invented a robotic lawnmower, but instead it had created a bald patch of soil in the middle of their back garden.

'But *this* is cutting edge,' smiled the professor, proud of his joke. 'It's guaranteed to smarten you up. One day, everyone will be getting their hair cut with one of these. It's got different settings, so we'll start with something light.'

'Go on, Dad,' urged Ben. 'Be a trailblazer.'

'Do it, Dad,' agreed Sophie and Ollie together.

Mrs Cook remained silent.

'Go for it,' woofed Spud.

Dad took the blue helmet and looked inside.

'You can't see anything,' said the professor. 'You place it on your head, press this button on the side to choose your style and away you go. All sorted in less than thirty seconds.'

Dad looked a little more impressed. 'Thirty seconds, eh?' he said, mulling it over. 'I do need a trim. Go on, then.'

'Yay!' yapped Star and Spud, excited to see a new gadget in action.

The professor helped fasten the strap. He pointed at the screen in the corner of the room. 'Which style?' he asked, clicking through a few pictures.

Dad grimaced as he whizzed through a Mohican, skinhead, Afro and ponytail.

'That one,' said Dad suddenly, as a famous James Bond actor appeared on screen. 'He's got cool hair and a modern style. I'll have a Bond look.'

Lara nodded approvingly.

The professor pushed his spectacles back to the

bridge of his nose and looked at the remote. In the professor's world, everyone and everything had a code name. 'That's a OO7,' he muttered, consulting the manual. He tapped a few numbers into the keypad on the side of the helmet. 'And I'll set the level to "light trim". Right — all programmed. We're good to go. You ready, Mr Cook?'

'Yes, are you *sure* you're ready?' asked Mum, giving one of her stern looks.

'As I'll ever be,' smiled Dad, avoiding eye contact. 'What do I have to do?'

'Just sit down,' said the professor. 'And keep your head still. It may feel slightly strange as the lasers get to work, but it'll all be over in a few seconds.'

Lasers? winced Lara.

Dad sat down, his neck straight, a serious look of concentration on his face. Sophie stifled a giggle.

The professor pressed another button and put his thumbs up. 'And go,' he said.

The helmet whirred into action and Mr Cook started to giggle. 'It tickles!' he said.

'Really?' said the professor, 'Hmm, well this

is only a prototype, remember. Still experimental,' he added, as all eyes watched Dad.

Dad's smile disappeared, replaced by a look of concern. 'Experimental?' he asked. 'You mean it's not safe?'

'Oh, it's safe, Mr Cook, don't worry about that. But sometimes the styles don't work out *quite* like the picture.'

'Maybe you'll have a Mohican after all, Dad,'

suggested Ollie brightly. Mrs Cook turned slightly pale.

The whirring stopped and a green light appeared on the front of the helmet.

'All done,' smiled the professor, loosening the strap. 'Let's reveal the James Bond haircut.' Professor Cortex removed the helmet and this time Sophie couldn't stifle her giggle.

Mrs Cook looked horrified. Her hand went to her mouth in shock. 'What on earth –?'

'What?' said Dad, in a panic as he stood up and went over to the mirror. 'Argh!' he shrieked. What have you done to me?'

His lovely straight hair had been expertly permed. A mass of tight curls stood high on the top of his head. The sides were shaved. It was a most unusual look.

'He looks like a poodle,' barked Spud.

'It's not very 007, Dad,' admitted Ben. 'More OAP.'

'I did explain,' stuttered the professor, 'that it's still in development.'

'*After* you'd pressed Go,' yelled Dad, running his fingers through the curls. 'I look like James Bond's grandmother.'

Poodles are very intelligent, at least, thought Lara.

'It'll grow out, Dad,' smiled Ollie.

'Yes, don't worry,' said the professor, 'and you can always have another go to see if we can put it right.'

Dad glared. 'Are you a *nutty* professor? I'm not subjecting myself to that contraption again!'

Sophie clapped enthusiastically. 'It's a great idea,' she said. 'Just needs tweaking. What else have you got, Professor?'

'Lots, young lady,' he continued. 'But now something for spies. Which one of you little fellas wants this?' he asked the puppies, holding up a small dog collar.

Spud raised his paw. Star raised hers higher, her claws straining for the ceiling.

Pick me, Prof, she urged. *Please pick me for a gadget collar.*

The professor knelt down beside Star and demonstrated his new device. 'Basic,' he said, 'but highly effective. This collar has a small button. Here,' he said, pushing his glasses up to the bridge of his nose to get a closer look. 'Press it and it releases a dart – laced with a truth drug. Victims will confess to any crimes they've committed, no matter how small.'

How cool is that? thought Star, her neck lengthening with pride. She eyed her brother suspiciously. *I wonder if I can aim it at him to see if he stole my last custard cream?*

'Anything for me, Prof?' wagged Spud.

'And don't worry, young fella,' beamed the professor. 'I've got something very special for you too.' The professor held up another collar and Spud's tail sprang into life. 'Yours is even more special. Same button and same dart. But this one's tipped with my brand-new memory-loss formula. It's completely fabulous. Watch this.' He turned and waved to his colleague across the office. 'Hello, Brian,' he shouted.

The man waved back and smiled. 'See,' said the professor under his breath. 'His name's not even Brian. It's Nigel! The chap's totally confused and will remain so for a whole week. I have to give him a lift home every night. He can't even remember where he lives!'

'Wow!' said Ollie. 'Maybe we could use it on Dad so he forgets how he used to look?'

'Your father is banned from testing another gadget ever again!' said Mrs Cook sternly, glaring at the professor.

Spud wagged his tail proudly. 'I can't wait to get a chance to use it on a bad guy!'

'Keep it away from me, son,' yapped Lara. 'I need my brain in top condition!'

'Right, no time for any more inventions, folks,' finished Professor Cortex. 'I have some final business for GM451 and the spy pups.' He lowered his head and peered over the top of his spectacles. 'This is top secret,' he said, tapping the side of his nose. 'That is, if they fancy a daring adventure?'

5. Resistance is Futile

Spud cocked his head, his eyes shining with excitement. Star's tail beat a rhythm on the floor. 'An adventure? Like a real mission? Do we fancy one? What do you think?'

Lara looked rather concerned. She cast a warning glance at the professor. *This had better not be anything serious*, she thought. *We're family pets first and foremost.*

Mrs Cook sighed. 'I don't think so, Professor,' she said sternly. 'We've had nothing but excitement and danger since we adopted Lara.' She pointed at Spud. 'He's already got a bullet hole in his ear – just like Lara's! There's no way I'm risking the dogs or the children ever again. I'm not allowing them to be involved in one of your special missions.'

'Quite,' agreed the professor. 'But you see,

Mrs Cook, this is a zero-risk project. But I totally understand if you don't want the pups to solve a crime spree that's been baffling the police for years. Not just here, but across the world,' he added, his eyes sparkling. 'And I totally understand it if you don't want them to have their most exciting adventure to date. Or to have massive fun along the way. Even if there's no danger,' continued the professor. 'I understand your position.'

I wonder what that could be, thought Lara. *That sounds unlike any mission the professor has ever handed out before. Too good to be true?*

The puppies' jaws had dropped in amazement.

'Did he say an exciting adventure?' yapped Spud.

'With one hundred per cent fun and zero per cent danger?' wagged Star. 'It's a no-brainer! You have to let us, Ma,' begged Spud, putting on his pleading eyes for Lara. 'It sounds so exciting. And we'll be ever so careful – promise!'

Lara looked at the children and her puppies. They were longing for a nod. She glanced at Mr Cook, who was standing at the mirror pulling his hair down to attempt some ear coverage. *He's not even listening!* And finally at Mrs Cook, who was wearing her familiar stern face. *But she's very tuned in!*

Let's hear him out, she decided. Lara gave a doggie nod.

'Mum?' said Sophie hopefully.

Mrs Cook looked at the puppies' hopeful faces. She sighed. 'Let's hear what you've got to say, Professor,' she replied. 'But no danger – you promised.'

The children and pups exploded with delight.

'OK,' said the professor, 'here's the puzzle.'

Clarissa White had been doing her homework on the Cooks' home town. She was a wanted woman and everyone had been reluctant to give her the information she so desperately needed. But that was OK because she loved using force.

'I'm sorry about this,' she lied, clutching a pair of pliers.

A man stood in front of her, blood streaming from his mouth. He held his teeth in his hand. His eyes were wild with terror.

'Would you be so kind,' she purred, 'as to avoid spilling your blood on my white carpet?' She passed him a towel and he held it to his mouth. 'If you'd have just given me the information first time round, we'd have had no need to use these,' she said, holding the tool aloft. 'That's your teeth gone, but I can work on fingernails too . . .'

The man gulped. His eyes, already revealing panic, were now watering.

'So where are the diamonds?' she hissed. 'I want the location of the best haul of diamonds in town.'

The man's resistance had gone from ten to zero. His eyes darted around – before coming to rest on the pliers. 'The Parthingthonth's,' he said, spitting out more blood. 'They liff in the big houth. Got at leath a dothen thparklerth. Betht diamonth in town.'

'Partingtons?' asked the lady, emphasising the 't's.

'Yeth, Parthingthonth,' he confirmed.

Clarissa White scribbled the name on a pad. 'Where?'

'The manor. Fourth floor,' surrendered the man. 'In the thafe.'

Clarissa White looked pleased. 'Thank you, Ivan,' she said. 'That will be all.'

The bloodied man was led away and Clarissa White reached for her mobile. She texted 'Partington Manor' and clicked Send.

6. A Man with a Plan

The Cook family gathered in the professor's office. He swept the mess off the table and booted up his laptop. Spud jumped on to Sophie's knee and Star snuggled up with Ollie. Ben scratched behind Lara's ear as Mum and Dad stood nervously, Dad still tugging at his perm. The wall lit up as an image was projected on to it.

'Diamonds,' began the professor. 'And rubies and emeralds. Millions of pounds' worth of them have gone missing. From towns across the country. It seems the robbers simply pick a town and empty it of its gems.' A picture of a diamond was beamed on to the wall. 'The police have nicknamed them the "Roving Robbers" because they've swept through the country. What makes this crime so unusual is

that cash is never taken. Often, after the thief
has broken into the safe, there is a massive wad
of notes alongside the stones. The cash is just
left. As if they're simply not interested in
money.'

'Why would that be?' thought Ben aloud.
'Why just take the jewels?'

'Why, indeed,' nodded the professor. 'The
police are baffled. And there's another unusual
angle to this spate of crimes,' he added, clicking
a button on his laptop. 'There's never a forced
entry. No sign of a break-in whatsoever. This
is the *tidiest* criminal – or criminals – ever. So
how does the robber enter and exit without
being noticed? Even the CCTV footage has
failed to show anyone breaking in or out.'

'Very strange,' agreed Dad. 'So do the police
have any suspects?'

The professor adopted what he imagined to

be his best mysterious face. 'Just one suspect, sir,' he said dramatically, revealing the next picture.

All eyes went to the wall, where there was a picture of a glamorous lady in white. Her cat was staring straight at the camera, its eyes illuminated in red. 'Clarissa White,' said the professor. 'One very evil lady.'

With an evil cat, thought Star.

She's an infamous jewel thief,' explained Professor Cortex. 'Current whereabouts unknown. But police believe she's still active. We think she's the brains behind this series of thefts. She's unspeakably horrible. It's possible she's not the actual thief on this occasion, but is pulling the strings on the project from behind the scenes.'

'Any more clues?' asked Sophie.

'Oh yes,' chirped the professor. 'Get a load of this. He clicked the laptop once more and a huge big top was beamed on to the wall.

'A circus!' marvelled Ollie. 'That's such a cool clue.'

'Cool clue, indeed, Master Oliver. This is the only link between all the burglaries,' added the professor, in what he now deemed to be his best Sherlock Holmes style. 'They've all taken place when the circus is in town. Of course, once they worked it out, the police had the circus watched. Searched, even. But nothing. Zilch. Zero. No gems. No sign of crime at all. But the police still think there's a link between Clarissa White and this circus.' The professor reflected on a lot of puzzled faces.

'So what kind of circus is it?' asked Ben.

'The old-fashioned sort, unfortunately,' said the professor, clicking again. 'But that may just help us.'

'Hmm,' said Lara suspiciously. 'I hope that doesn't mean any animals are in trouble!'

A man in a red coat and top hat was beamed on to the screen.

'Awesome eyebrows!' cooed Ollie.

'This is Tony Jewell. Owner, ringmaster and, by all accounts, dreadful chap,' said Professor Cortex. 'Shouts a lot. Bullies people. Nasty man. And yes, Oliver, extraordinary eyebrows. But that doesn't make him a criminal.'

Spud let out a low growl. 'I don't like him. Not if he shouts at people.'

'And here's his wife, Jennifer Jewell. Lovely lady. From what we can make out, she's the opposite of her husband. And here are a few of the performers and animals,' continued the professor, clicking rapidly through a few slides.

Lara, the pups and the children gasped at some of the pictures.

'A bearded lady!' woofed Star, amazed.

Ollie nearly fell off his seat when he saw the trapeze artist. 'We definitely need to get involved with this one,' he said. 'It'd be *so* exciting to visit the circus.'

'But the elephant and lions are not so exciting,' yapped Spud. 'That's cruel!'

'It's more than *visiting*,' noted the professor. 'I want the puppies to *infiltrate* the circus.'

'What's *infiltrate*?' asked Ollie.

'Spy on!' said Ben, his eyes shining.

Star looked at her brother and their tails started to wag faster than ever.

'And next week we have the perfect opportunity,' explained Professor Cortex, 'because the circus will be in *our* town. They're setting up the big top in the park as we speak.'

'So the robberies will probably happen here!' yelled Ben. 'We have to investigate, Mum,' he said, his eyes pleading like the puppies sometimes did.

'Obviously, I don't want to subject the pups to undue risk,' coughed the professor. 'But we need to find the robbers so they will lead us to Clarissa White or whoever is behind these crimes. The circus is holding an open day this Sunday – they have this thing where they invite some local people to take part in one of the acts. Drums up a bit of local interest and helps build a bigger crowd. I was rather hoping the pups might go along and get talent-spotted. Then they'll be able to perform with the circus for a week. Sort of undercover, I suppose – proper spy-pup work, but without any real risk because they're allowed to be there. They can do some careful observing, see what they can find and then report back to either myself or the police.'

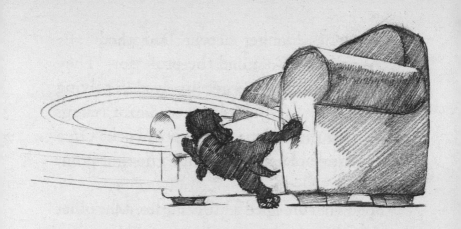

Spud was off around the room, tail wagging, dancing on his hind legs. He shadow-boxed. 'Take that, you baddie diamond robber,' he said. 'And one for good luck,' he said, kicking the sofa.

Star had her nose to the carpet, sniffing hard, bloodhound-style. 'And I'll be finding clues,' she woofed. 'This powerful *sch*noz will find any gems that may be hidden.'

'Just think,' said Ben. 'If the circus gets closed down, then all the animals will be saved too!'

I like the sound of that, thought Lara.

'The pups look keen,' said Sophie. 'Can they, Mum? Can they become a circus act and go on an exciting mission?'

The colour had drained from Mum's cheeks. She sat limply.

'What's the danger factor?' Dad asked.

'Almost zero,' smiled the professor. 'They don't actually have to get involved in solving anything. They're just observers. Learn a circus skill, join the troupe and report back. On a danger scale of one to ten, it's a nought point five.'

Spud's tail drooped a little. He liked the other end of the spectrum.

'Well,' sighed Mum, 'I suppose if it's just the pups, and the kids aren't doing the snooping . . . and it's going to stop a *local* robbery. And it involves diamonds! Then it has to be a yes.'

Pandemonium broke out among the children and dogs.

'So long as everyone's *very* careful,' she shouted above the hullabaloo. 'And we can get free tickets to keep an eye on them during the show! Deal?'

'Deal!' said the professor. 'Let the adventure begin.'

7. *Judgement Day*

Spud and Star had hardly slept and arrived bright and early at the circus auditions with Ben, Sophie and Ollie. A huge crowd began to gather, with quite a few people practising their acrobatic and juggling skills. At 10.00 a.m. Tony Jewell emerged from his caravan and stood on a stage to address the crowd.

'Good morning,' he bellowed in his best ringmaster's voice. 'Welcome to my circus. As you know, we have the finest performers in the world,' he exaggerated. 'But today we intend to choose just one act. We are on the hunt for locals. The finest, most gifted that this town has to offer. And they will be performing in this week's shows.'

The crowd applauded warmly. Each person was issued with a numbered sticker and instructed

to perform their potential circus act. Tony Jewell and a few of the performers wandered among the crowd, making notes. A tap on the shoulder meant you were out. The performers soon thinned.

Ollie got an early tap for his rubbish dance routine. Sophie's mime act was also rather amateurish, so she was relieved to be asked to sit down. Finally, Ben and the puppies put their plan into action.

'Let's show them what we've got,' yapped Spud excitedly.

'Here goes,' Ben said as he saw Tony Jewell approaching. He took the three juggling balls from his pocket and prepared to throw them in the air. The puppies sat patiently, waiting for the ringmaster to glance their way.

'Now,' woofed Spud, eyeing the circus owner. 'He's coming over.'

Ben threw the three balls high into the air and

sat down. Spud put his paws together and caught the first one, tossing it straight back into the sky. Star took charge of ball number two and before they knew it, the three balls were being juggled backwards and forwards between the puppies.

'Check us out,' woofed Spud. 'The world's most talented pups.'

'Mum's taught us well,' barked Star. 'We can ride bikes too, you know.'

The rest of the performers stopped and watched in amazement. Star finished by catching a ball on the end of her nose and flicking it into a nearby dustbin. Spud volleyed his final ball into the air, twizzled and caught it on the back of his neck like he'd seen Premiership footballers do.

Ta-daaa, he thought.

Star curtseyed and Spud bowed as they listened to the applause of the audience.

Tony Jewell's bushy eyebrows were raised in delight. 'Wow,' he exclaimed. 'I think we have something very special here today.' He looked at Ben. 'Could I work with your dogs and put them on stage tonight?'

Ben grinned widely. He winked at the puppies. *You're in!*

'Mr Jewell,' he said, 'it would be an honour.'

Once the auditions were over the local people were shooed away and the puppies were put in the care of Tony Jewell to do an hour's practice. There was no time for snooping.

The professor was right – Tony Jewell was a hard man. The ringmaster barked orders to everyone and all the other performers seemed scared of him. As soon as Ben was out of earshot he yelled at the puppies and even aimed a kick at Star.

'I hate dogs,' he snarled. 'The last thing we need is a pair of flea-bitten mongrels in the show, even if you can juggle. But if you draw in some extra customers, then I have no choice.'

Star bared her teeth and issued a low warning growl. 'And I don't much like you either, mister,' she growled. 'Tony Jewell-Thief. I hope we catch you red-handed.'

8. The Parade

Tony Jewell had arranged a mid-afternoon parade through the town, which gave the performers a chance to show off their skills and the circus an opportunity to gain some free publicity and sell tickets. The puppies were bundled on to the back of a lorry and were expected to sit and wave a paw at the crowds as they drove by.

They had to admit it was a wonderful carnival atmosphere. The lorry also had some acrobats who were wowing the crowd, and a clown with ridiculous shoes and a huge flower in his button hole. Every time someone from the audience asked to smell the flower, they received a squirt of water for their troubles. Spud thought this was hilarious. They also shared the lorry with Gordon Gibbons the monkey trainer. He had a pair of identical monkeys: small, brown and very cheeky.

At least they're not chained up, thought Spud.

In fact, the red-coated primates were expert pickpockets and would scamper into the crowd and return with some earrings, a watch or bracelet. Gordon would then grin and hold up the wares for the unsuspecting owner to claim.

Star was on alert. *Another suspect!* She couldn't help wondering if that was how the jewels were being stolen, but Gordon was giving everything back, so she dismissed the idea. *But I'll be keeping an eye on you and your monkeys*, she thought.

The parade was a huge success. Crowds cheered and waved. At the end, two free tickets were given away in a spectacular manner. The circus stopped outside the largest house in town, Partington Manor. Tony Jewell rang the bell and the crowd that was following the procession hushed as they waited for an answer. Gordon sent his monkeys over the wall to see what was going on and eventually the gates glided open and Lord and Lady Partington stood, beaming and waving. The crowd applauded. Tony Jewell called for hush and he gave Lord and Lady Partington two tickets for the circus' closing-night extravaganza. He declared the week a total sell-out and the crowd erupted once more.

Lara couldn't help but be a little worried. *The professor said it was a zero-danger mission, but I still don't like it.* Lara had tangled with jewel thieves before. *And they can be very dangerous indeed!* She had stood with the children while the parade went by and then followed the throng to Partington Manor. The retired spy dog scanned the crowd as they cheered, her expert eyes searching for anything out of the ordinary. *The problem is,* she thought, *that with circus performers, everything's out of the ordinary!*

'Good job we've got our tickets, Lara,' shouted Ben as the last pair were given away to Lord and Lady Partington. 'But I'll tell the professor that they need to keep the Manor under surveillance on Saturday night. Inviting the richest couple in town to the closing night sounds like a trap.'

Lara nodded. *I'll just be glad when the show's over and the pups come home*, she thought.

Spud and Star returned to the circus having thoroughly enjoyed their afternoon and were now looking forward to the evening show. Spud satisfied his appetite with three toffee apples, a burger and two bundles of candyfloss.

The pups were put in the care of Gordon Gibbons. He gave them some straw to bed down in. 'Relax, pups,' he said. 'Get some rest. We need a big performance from you this evening.'

Great idea, thought Spud, licking candyfloss from his face. He lay down for a snooze while his sister sneaked out of their caravan to do some spy-pup investigations. 'Be careful, sis,' he said sleepily.

Star crept under the canvas and into the big

top. *Think like a spy pup*, she told herself. *And stay out of sight*.

The circus was alive with performers practising their routines. There were just two hours to go before the evening show. The tightrope team were balancing high above. Star crept past the lion's cage, rather pleased that he was asleep. The strongman was ripping up telephone directories and the fire-eater was oiling his mouth. Star sat and watched as the rubber man practised his routine. He stood on a small box and bowed to the imaginary crowd. Then he opened the box and held it up so the audience could see just how tiny it was. Star watched in disbelief as he then stretched himself tall, his arms held high, and twisted his hands together in what looked like a very awkward way. His bones cracked and his shoulders went bendy.

Yikes, he's deliberately dislocated his shoulders!

The rubber man then proceeded to scrunch himself into the box.

There's no way, Star thought as he crouched in the very small box. *I mean, the box is tiny and he's tall. He's defying the laws of physics!*

The rubber man shuffled himself lower. He bent double.

Almost triple!

Finally, he lowered his head and his assistant flipped the lid shut.

Now that's quite a trick! marvelled Star, clapping her paws together in admiration. *Squeezing into tight places like that would be perfect for a burglar*, she noted.

After that, the spy pup lingered near the clowns as they perfected their routine.

What a cool car, she thought as they drove it into the big top in readiness for the evening's show. It was like a mini fire engine with a ladder on the back, but open-topped so the clowns could jump in and out as well as throw things at the crowd. It was mayhem. Star watched as the car drove around the circus ring with a clown hanging off the ladder. Star decided she'd like to train to be a clown.

It looks such great fun!

Night was coming and soon the locals would be turning up for an evening at the circus. Star had sniffed around, but could find no sign of crime. She watched as a lady strolled out of the big top back to her caravan.

She looks nice, thought Star as the lady bent down to stroke her.

'Oh, you're so cute,' she beamed. 'My husband's told me about you and your brother. You are the juggling pups.' Star rolled over for a tummy tickle.

And I like you too, she thought.

'Why don't you come with me for a biscuit?' said Jennifer Jewell.

Star thought this was a great idea. 'My bro stuffed his face at lunchtime, but I've not had a morsel,' she wagged. 'So a custard cream would be perfect.' She followed the lady back to her caravan.

Mrs Jewell flicked on the kettle. She smiled at

Star as she went about her business. 'We used to have a dog,' she said, not knowing that Star could understand every word, 'Tony and I. But he got too old to perform and Tony got rid of him.'

Yes, I've heard he's not very nice, thought Star. *He aimed a kick at me earlier! He'd better watch out or I'll get my mum on him!*

Star sat, ears upright as she heard the crinkling of a packet being opened. She sniffed the air. *Digestives! Nice one, Mrs J.* She tried to look cute. The lady broke a biscuit in half and threw it to her. Star expertly caught it and chomped the biscuit down in one. *Yummy! And the other half?*

'So now I busy myself making costumes,' explained Jennifer.

Star looked around. There were sparkly costumes hanging up everywhere. *And tubes of glitter and boxes of coloured beads. It's like Aladdin's cave!* thought Star.

'And I've got just the thing for you and your juggling sidekick.' The lady reached into a cupboard and brought out a sparkly cape. 'I've just made them,' she smiled. 'Made-to-measure circus outfits so when you enter the ring tonight, you'll look like *real* circus performers.'

'No way!' woofed Star. 'How thrilling!' The puppy lifted her head to allow Mrs Jewell to fasten the strap round her neck. Then she checked herself in the mirror. Her cloak sparkled and she looked like a real performer. The cape billowed out as she did a doggie twirl. 'I look like a superhero! This is the coolest thing ever. Thank you so much, Mrs Jewell.' She licked the lady's hand.

Jennifer Jewell threw the other half of the biscuit to Star and it disappeared the same way as the first. 'Tony's decided to introduce you as "The Precious Puppies", which you most certainly are.' She smiled.

Star licked her lips before taking Spud's outfit in her mouth and bounding outside. She trotted proudly across the field back to her brother. *Wait till he sees his new sparkly outfit*, she thought. *Tonight 'The Precious Puppies' will steal the show!*

9. Bat Dog

Clarissa White sat in her castle watching the fish. She was irritated that she'd heard nothing from Tony Jewell. She pressed a button and the speakerphone sprang into life. The ringmaster had obviously recognized the number because he sounded nervous. 'Hello there,' he began. 'How are —'

'No need for niceties,' she snapped. 'I gave you one week, Tony,' she reminded him. 'And that was exactly one week ago.'

'Everything's scheduled for this Saturday,' stammered the ringmaster. 'Partington Manor, like you said. You'll have your gems soon enough.'

'Saturday's no good, Tony,' she purred, her evilness somehow sounding silky. 'Tomorrow is delivery day. Bring your plan forward. The robbery happens tonight.' Miss White left a deathly pause. 'Consider this your last warning.'

'Yes, but –' began the ringmaster.

The line went dead. Clarissa White smiled at her cat. 'We get more diamonds tomorrow,' she smiled, fingering the cat's collar. 'Or the fish will be getting very well fed.'

It was one hour until the first show of the week. Star watched as Tony Jewell took a call on his mobile. She couldn't help but notice that he went grey. *Somebody must have delivered some bad news*. He pocketed his phone and looked for someone to bellow at. Unfortunately for them, the pups were practising their juggling and dropped a ball just as the ringmaster was striding by. *Whoops*, thought Spud.

The circus owner shook his head and cursed. 'Stupid good-for-nothing dogs,' he yelled. 'I knew we should have chosen people. If you two don't get your act together you'll find yourselves locked up over there,' he threatened.

Spud followed his finger and gulped. 'Lion!' he woofed to his sister. 'Let's practise a bit harder.'

But Star didn't want to practise. Tony Jewell

marched off to shout at another act. 'Come on, bro,' she woofed. 'We're not here to perform. This is a spying mission – remember? We have to snoop. There may be millions of pounds' worth of diamonds hidden somewhere. And it's our job to sniff them out!'

'But what about him?' barked her brother, jabbing his paw at the ringmaster. 'He's going to feed us to the lion.'

'He wouldn't dare,' replied Star. 'And besides,

we'll have Mum here later and she won't take any nonsense. It may be Mr Eyebrows who gets fed to the lions!'

'OK,' said Spud. 'But let's be quick before he comes back.'

The pups scooted out of the big top and scampered from caravan to caravan, listening at doors and windows.

'Hide!' yapped Star as she spotted the rubber man walking across the field towards them.

They hid under a red lorry as he went past, talking on his mobile. 'We're all ready for Saturday,' he muttered. He listened to his mobile for a few seconds. 'OK,' they heard him say, 'but this is my final act. I'll take my cut, and run.'

Spud and Star looked at each other in shock. 'Did you hear that?' whined Spud. 'Maybe he's one of the criminals?'

'Saturday?' replied Star. 'That's the night the Partingtons are supposed to come for the closing night. Ben said the prof will have police all over their manor house. Looks like this could be the end of their stealing spree, sis!'

The dogs kept their eye on the man as he sauntered away across the field. He was joined by one of the tightrope walkers. The pair looked around, a little suspiciously, before entering the ringmaster's caravan. Star beckoned to her brother. 'Let's check it out.' The puppies lolloped across the field to the biggest caravan. Star cocked her head, straining to hear. 'No good. We need to get up to that window,' she woofed, jabbing her paw upwards. 'But how?'

The puppies looked around. Spectators were now arriving and the place was getting busy. The clowns were squirting people as they entered the big top. The candyfloss seller was doing a roaring trade and there was a line of children queuing to feed the elephant, who looked tired of eating peanuts.

'There's a skylight on the top of the caravan,' woofed Star. 'So if I can get on the roof I can probably listen in.' Both pups looked up at the caravan towering above them.

'Look, here's our chance!' yapped Star, pointing a paw at the clown car that was driving their way. 'If I can get on the car, I can leap on to the caravan roof as it drives by.'

Spud looked unsure. 'Sounds risky,' he woofed. *Mrs Cook wouldn't like it one bit,* he thought.

'Of course it's risky,' said his sister in frustration. 'But we're spy pups. We sometimes have to live by the seat of our pants. You just stop the car and I'll do the rest.'

The clown car was nearly upon them. *No time to think!* Spud ran out in front of the car, stood on his hind legs and put his paws in the air. He felt like a highwayman! 'Hold it there!' he barked in his loudest voice. 'And please stop or I'm a flattened pup!'

The clown driver saw the puppy and hit the

brake pedal. The comedy car lurched to a halt and the clown jumped out. 'You stupid little mutt!' he began. 'You could have got yourself squashed –' Then he looked around at the spectators, who'd gathered to watch, and realized he needed to be clowning not moaning. He softened and forced a smile. 'But, little fella, it's a good job I saw you in time.' The clown picked Spud up, stroked his head and moved him away from the wheels. He got back in his car and started up the engine. Then with a big honk of the horn and a wave to the crowd, he drove off towards the big top.

Star had taken advantage of the situation. She'd timed it just right and jumped up on to the car bonnet and then on to the ladder. As the clown car drove by the caravan, she leapt like a cat and scrabbled on to the caravan roof.

Phew! That was close. She waved at her brother below and then padded silently across the caravan roof to the skylight. *Excellent, it's open.*

Star hung down like a bat and peeped in. *I need to lower myself in for a better view.* Her ears dangled full length, swaying as she scrabbled to hold herself in place with her back paws.' *It's a bit uncomfortable, but it'll have to do.*

Tony Jewell and his gang were sitting at the kitchen table. The rubber man was drawing something and everyone else was poring over the picture. 'You're sure it's on the fourth floor?' asked the tightrope lady.

'Course I'm sure,' said Gordon the monkey man. 'The monkeys have scouted it. And sorted it. Cameras are off. We're all set.'

Star couldn't believe her doggie ears. *So some of the animals are being used as criminal spies! This is getting very interesting indeed*. Her ears were fully extended, soaking up the conversation. *Perfect for spying!*

'Anything, sis?' yapped Spud from outside. 'Any clues?'

Star heaved herself out of the skylight and leant over the end of the caravan. '*Shush*,' she whined, putting her paw to her lips. 'Plenty going on, bro. I think we may have found our robbers.' She resumed her half-dog, half-bat position, ears swinging gently. Nobody noticed the puppy's head peering in at the kitchen table.

'And when do the old codgers arrive?' asked the rubber man.

'I've rung the Partingtons personally and asked if they could come for the opening night instead. They've got front-row tickets, so are guaranteed to be here. Probably in their seats already,' said Tony Jewell. 'Remember, we've promised Clarissa a million. Anything less and we're for it.' Star watched as Tony Jewell ran his finger across his neck. 'She wants the gems tomorrow so there's no margin for error.'

Stars eyes widened. *Tonight? But the Partingtons weren't supposed to come until Saturday.*

'So what time do we strike?' asked the acrobat.

'Very soon,' said the ringmaster, glancing at his watch. 'Those ridiculous clowns are on first. Then Lenny and his lion. Then "The Precious Puppies" to impress the locals, so we've got a clear forty minutes before any of you perform. Wait for the intro, wave to the crowd, then we're away. Lord and Lady Partington won't know a thing.'

The blood had started to rush to Star's head. Her eyes were bulging. Her back legs wobbled a bit and she panicked. The effort of pulling herself back on to the roof was too much. *I'm stuck,* she thought. *Upside down, like a bat!* She felt the blood pumping in her face. Her back legs wobbled a bit more and she felt herself slipping. *Uh-oh! Not good!*

There was a resounding *crash* as the puppy
hit the floor. Cats are famous for landing on
their feet; unfortunately, dogs are not. Star lay
on the caravan floor, winded and in pain. The
conversation stopped and all eyes turned
towards her.

'Hi, guys,' she gasped in a weird puppy woof.
'Just thought I'd drop in.'

10. Hot Pursuit

Spud watched as the caravan door was hauled open and his sister was thrown out.

'And stay out!' bellowed Tony Jewell. There was a terrified yowl and Star landed with a *thud*. Spud galloped to check on his sister.

'You OK, sis?' he panted, planting a wet slurp across her face.

Star stood up gingerly. She rolled her head from side to side until they heard a *click*. 'That's better,' she woofed.

'What did you find out?' asked her brother, his tail swishing. 'Any clues?'

'*Major* clues! We were right that they're the criminals, but the plans have changed,' gasped Star. 'The Partingtons are coming *tonight*, so the robbery kicks off in a few minutes!'

'*What?*' yelped Spud. 'But the police are

ready for Saturday! We've got to warn the professor!'

The caravan door opened and the criminal gang poured out, with Tony Jewell in the lead. The rubber man reached down and scooped up Spud. 'Are you two pups still on the loose?' he sneered. 'You've got a crowd to entertain.'

'You too, mutt,' added the monkey man, grabbing Star roughly by the scruff of her neck and heading off towards the big top. 'It's showtime, Precious Puppies.'

There wasn't a moment to call for help. The pups waited nervously backstage. They had their sparkly

capes on and Jennifer Jewell had given them some sunglasses to complete their stage look. Spud had checked himself in every mirror.

Pretty cool, he admitted. *Even if I say so myself.*

The other performers were stretching their muscles and wishing each other good luck. The show was about to begin.

The problem is, so's the robbery! Star peeped out from behind the curtain at the packed crowd. Lord and Lady Partington were sitting in the VIP seats in the front row. Star saw the Cook family and Professor Cortex and waved. Ollie spotted her and gave her a thumbs up.

Spud tried to point to the Partingtons, but the professor just waved back.

'We have to get a message to the prof,' woofed Star. 'There's a huge robbery happening in the next thirty minutes! What are we going to do?'

Spud didn't have time to answer. The puppies were dragged into the centre of the ring, along with all the other performers. The spotlight picked out Tony Jewell, in top hat and Union Jack waistcoat, who puffed his chest out with pride as he introduced the show.

He's terrible, thought Spud. *So many fibs about*

how funny the clowns are. I've seen them practise and Mr Cook's new hairstyle is more amusing than them.

The performers left the stage to huge applause, leaving the clowns and their wobbly fire engine to start the show. Spud and Star strained to see where the gang had gone. Star spotted the tightrope walker disappearing out of a tent flap.

'Quick,' she woofed, 'let's get the professor and give chase!'

Star checked all around, looking for a way out. There was a small gap under the big top and she went for it.

'This way, bro. Too big for a person, but just right for a spy pup.' Star fell to her tummy and squeezed out into the night air. The pups sprinted round the marquee to the entrance.

'Mum!' said Spud, spotting Lara sitting outside. She got to her feet.

'*Mum, Mum, robbers!*' howled Star. 'Robbers on the loose! They're going to steal the jewels from Lord and Lady Partington *tonight*,' she panted.

'We have to stop them,' gasped Spud, 'before Tony Jewell notices we're missing!'

'We sure do,' Lara barked. She knew there was no time to waste. *But I think we'll need the professor's help*, she thought. *He's got a mobile so he can ring the police. The problem is, he's in there and dogs aren't allowed in.* Lara stuck her head through the big top entrance and scanned the crowd. Ben, Sophie and Ollie were applauding the clowns. Lara put her paw in her doggie mouth and did her best whistle. 'Over here, Prof, we need your help!' But the noise of the band was too loud. She tried again and Ben looked up. He saw Lara waving her paws about and knew something was up. He nudged his brother and sister.

'Look. Lara wants us. Come on, guys, Let's scram.'

'Just going to get a drink,' said Ben as he stood and pushed past their mum and dad.

'Me too,' said Sophie. 'All this laughing's making me thirsty!'

'And don't forget me,' piped up their younger brother.

'Go easy on the fizz, Ollie,' warned Mum. 'You're excited enough as it is.'

The children filed out of their row and through the tent flap into the cool evening air. The sound of the performance was muffled and the smell of hot dogs wafted past.

'What is it, Lara?' asked Sophie. 'Is it the baddies? Have you caught them?'

'It is the baddies,' nodded Lara. 'But we haven't caught them yet.' Lara barked instructions to the pups. 'You go to Partington Manor to keep an eye on proceedings. I'll stay here in case the baddies return this way. Don't take any risks, OK? Follow them, observe and report back here.'

'OK, Ma,' saluted Star.

'Understood,' agreed Spud.

The pups bounded off into the night. Lara looked at the *No Dogs* sign that was hanging at the entrance to the big top. *This is an emergency*, she decided as she bounded inside to fetch the professor.

The three Cook children looked at each other, bewildered. 'What's going on?' asked Ollie.

'What was all that barking about?' said Sophie. 'What do we do?'

They looked at Ben. He shrugged. 'Seems to be more action that-a-way,' he smiled, pointing after Spud and Star.

'An adventure!' yelped Ollie, and the children ran off in pursuit of the puppies.

11. Escape Route

The pups scampered as fast as their short legs would carry them. The gate to Partington Manor was locked. They noticed a ladder up against the wall. 'That must be their way into the grounds,' yapped Spud. 'But we don't need that.' The puppies fell to their bellies and crept underneath the gate, Spud instantly regretting the toffee apples earlier. He got stuck halfway and his sister had to give his collar a tug. Spud dusted himself off and they surveyed the scene.

'Wow, it really is a mansion! Over there,' said Star, jabbing a paw towards the front of the house. The puppies crept into a nearby bush.

'Look,' whispered Spud, pointing at three of the circus performers who'd gathered on the doorstep. The tightrope walker and the rubber man were discussing something. Gordon Gibbons was giving the monkeys a banana to keep them quiet.

How are they going to get in? wondered Star. *I guess their secret will be revealed.*

Spud yelped with fear as someone grabbed his collar. 'There you are,' whispered Ben. The children had scaled the ladder and joined the puppies in the shadows. All eyes fell on the small gang of robbers. 'What now?' mouthed Ben to the pups.

They watched as the rubber man went through a few stretches and then raised his arms high above his head. He twisted in a very awkward way and

Sophie let out a small squeal as the rubber man dislocated his shoulders and started to feed himself, feet first, through the cat flap. 'No way!' said Sophie, peering through her fingers. 'He'll never be able to squeeze through that tiny hole.'

She was wrong. It took a lot of wriggling, but eventually the thief was inside the manor. He spent two minutes putting his bones back in the right places and disabling the burglar alarm and then the door opened and in went the gang. The children heard the rubber man adopt a posh voice and say, 'Welcome to Partington Manor. Do come in and help yourself to whatever you want.' The other two laughed.

'We have to stop them,' Spud said to his sister, 'but Mum said not to do anything except watch.' He looked at Star.

'But that's not what a real spy pup would do,' she said hopefully.

'You're right,' he agreed. 'If we let them get away, then the circus will roll on to the next town. Let's go!'

'I don't think the puppies are just going to sit here, do you?' Ben whispered to his brother and sister as the puppies stared towards the open door.

'No,' agreed Sophie. 'Maybe we could sneak up and lock them in a room until the police arrive.'

'We can't phone them until we're inside anyway – my mobile is charging at home,' Ben pointed out.

'C'mon, sis,' said Spud. 'No time to waste!'

Star led the way. The children and puppies crept across the lawn and stood by the side door. Spud peeked in through the cat flap. 'All clear,' he wagged. He and his sister crept inside. Ben creaked open the door and soon the children and puppies were standing in the hallway of the fabulous house.

'Wow!' gasped Ollie, looking at the paintings and vases. 'The Partingtons are very rich people!'

'Soon to be much less rich,' said Sophie. 'When those horrible performers have stolen the gems.'

'I heard them say it was the fourth floor,' woofed Star to her brother quietly. 'Come on, team, let's investigate.'

Star scampered up the first flight of carpeted stairs, leaving muddy paw prints as she went. Ben, Sophie and Ollie crept along, Ollie doing exaggerated tiptoes like he'd seen in cartoons.

He issued a very loud '*Shush*,' for effect. Sophie
waved her arms and did a much quieter '*Shush*,'
to her brother.

'This is serious, Ollie,' she whispered. Then
she turned to her elder brother. 'Shouldn't we
just wait? Or call the police or something?'

'What, and miss this adventure?' hissed Ben.
'No way. Come on, sis.'

Up and up they went. Spud now led the way,
tail as straight as a car aerial. Star followed, nose
to the ground, sniffing furiously.

The children and puppies came to a fourth-floor bedroom. Spud was pointing inside. 'In there, guys. They're opening the safe.'

The Cook children peered round the door. The tightrope lady was rifling through Lady Partington's jewellery box, picking out the jewel-encrusted earrings, necklaces and bracelets. Gordon Gibbons had removed a painting to reveal the Partingtons' safe. The children watched as he put on a set of headphones and attached a gadget to the safe. He frowned with concentration. The monkey trainer turned the knob left, then right a bit, then left and right again until there was a satisfying *click*. The robbers smiled and Gordon gave a thumbs up. He pulled the lever and the wall safe swung open. Sophie held her hand over her mouth to stifle the gasp. There were wads of cash inside. But the burglars didn't seem interested. Instead, they removed a small black bag, tied with a ribbon. Gordon beckoned the others to the bed. He sat down, untied the bow and emptied the contents of the bag into his hand. A dozen sparkling diamonds glistened.

Sophie's hand went to her mouth again and Ollie's eyes nearly popped out of his head. He stepped backwards in amazement, straight into a huge vase. There was a loud *clatter* as the vase fell sideways. It seemed like slow motion as it rolled across the carpet and thudded down the stairs to the landing below, making a big *thump* down each stair. Ollie was horrified.

'Whoops!' he smiled, trying to look innocent.

Ben took his brother and sister by the hand and started to run down the stairs. The puppies had other ideas.

'Come on, Spud, we have to protect the kids and let them get out!' The dogs ran into the bedroom, barking as loudly as they could.

'Maximum chaos, sister!' Spud bared his teeth in an attempt to look menacing. Both dogs had their hackles raised, looking as big and fierce as two cute puppies can. Spud stood on his hind legs and puffed out his sparkly cloak. 'Beware,' he growled. 'Spy pups are on the case!'

'It's just dogs,' said the monkey man. 'Those stupid puppies from the circus. They must have followed us. Let's stay calm and get this job finished.' He glanced across at his monkeys. 'Derek, Clive – get 'em.'

Spud took a step backwards. *I've never fought*

monkeys, he thought as the large one swung from the lampshade and grabbed his cloak. Before he knew what was happening, the monkey had ripped off his cape and returned to the light fitting, chattering and laughing at the puppy.

You like jewels, don't you? Spud remembered from the parade that afternoon. *Well, come and get this then.* He pinched a sparkly watch off the bed and disappeared out of the door. The monkeys screeched with horror and gave chase. Spud leapt on to the banister and started to slide. 'Whoa!' he woofed. 'This is fast!' The banister curved its way to the ground floor and Spud's challenge was to stay aboard. He gripped with all his paws, his ears flapping wildly.

Ouch, my bottom's getting warm, he thought as he whizzed past the second floor. *But this is better than a theme-park ride!* He made sure he kept hold of the watch as he careered ever faster towards the bottom. *But how exactly am I going to get off at the end?* The end of the banister approached and Spud closed his eyes as he flew at high speed.

Star bounded down the stairs after her brother. As she reached the ground floor she

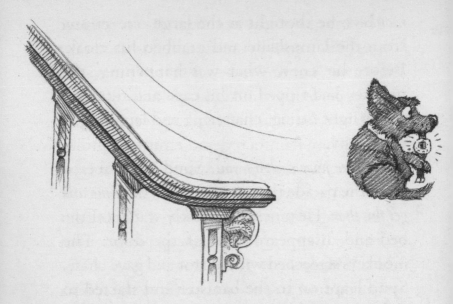

saw Spud lying in a heap, the evil monkeys circling him.

And now they're not cheeky, they're snarling, itching for a fight. Yikes! The monkeys eyed the watch hanging out of Spud's mouth. The puppy had recovered now and backed away, the monkeys inching forward.

Steady on, my primate pals, he thought. *Don't mess with me, I'm a black belt.* Spud backed into Lord Partington's office. He glanced around and spotted an open drawer in the filing cabinet. *Come and get it,* he teased as he jerked his head and tossed the sparkly watch into the open drawer.

The monkeys had been trained to retrieve jewels. They couldn't resist and both leapt for the drawer, fighting to be the first to the watch. With a perfectly timed karate kick, Star slid the drawer shut and the monkeys were trapped inside. They hammered and emitted muffled screeches, but the primates were out of action.

Star patted her paws together in satisfaction. 'Nice teamwork, bro,' she woofed. 'That's put an end to their monkey business! Now for the real baddies!'

The puppies bounded back up to the fourth floor and stood in the doorway. They watched as Gordon Gibbons pocketed the diamonds and clicked the safe shut. The tightrope lady closed the jewellery box. It was as though nobody had ever been in the bedroom.

Star went for the monkey man's ankles. She darted in and gave him a nasty nip.

'*Ouch!*' he yelled, hopping about. 'That dog bit me!' He kicked out, but Star dodged and his foot walloped a chair. '*Ouch!*' he yelled again. Not to be outdone, Spud grabbed his trouser leg and pulled the man off balance. He fell and cracked his head on the bedpost, then collapsed on to the floor.

'Out cold,' woofed Star. 'One down, two to go.'

The tightrope lady rummaged through Gordon Gibbons's pockets and retrieved the diamonds. Then she followed the rubber man out on to the landing and the pair galloped down the stairs, taking them three at a time. This wasn't going as smoothly as planned, but at least they had the diamonds.

Ben was waiting on the next landing, crouching behind a plant pot with Ollie and Sophie. He heard them coming and jumped out at exactly the right moment, pulling the trigger of a fire extinguisher. The rubber man was blasted with foam. Sophie threw the fire blanket over his head and Ollie pushed him down the next flight of stairs. He tumbled downwards with some agonizing crunches of bone. His rubber body wasn't expecting it and he landed awkwardly, breaking his ankle.

'*Owww!* My ankle! Mummy, it hurts,' he wailed, then went cross-eyed before slumping to the carpet, passing out from the pain.

'He's been extinguished,' yelled Ben. 'One baddie to go. Let's get her.' The tightrope lady had retreated back upstairs. She kicked her way past the snarling puppies and locked herself in the fourth-floor bedroom. The children and spy pups gathered outside.

Ben rattled the door handle. 'We're phoning the police!' he yelled. 'Hello, police,' he said loudly, pretending to be on the phone so the lady could hear. 'We've got a criminal tightrope walker locked in a room. Oh, and a rubber man and monkey trainer. We've captured them, red-handed, stealing jewels at Partington Manor. Please come quickly.'

He mouthed to his brother and sister. 'What do we do now?'

The lady sounded calm. 'The police won't be here in time,' she shouted back. 'I'm not hanging around to get caught. See you later, kids.'

'What does she mean?' asked Ollie. 'She can't escape from the fourth floor.'

Ben instructed Star to run for help. 'Go and fetch the professor,' he instructed. 'Not Mum or Dad, though. Especially not Mum,' he said, thinking of how she'd told them all to stay out of trouble. 'Star, you're the fastest. Now off you go.'

The puppy scampered down the stairs on a mission for help. But she was back thirty seconds later, her tongue hanging out of the side of her mouth. 'She's escaping,' woofed the puppy. 'She's tightrope-walking across to the next building. And the diamonds are escaping with her!'

12. Balancing Act

Star stood on her hind legs and mimed walking on a tightrope. She splayed her front legs and wobbled across an imaginary line on the carpet. *C'mon, guys, you know what this is.*

'No way,' yelled Ben. 'She's hot-footing it on a tightrope!' He grabbed the fire extinguisher and battered at the door. After four hefty blows the lock gave way and he fell into the bedroom. The group crowded round the window to see that the tightrope lady was indeed making her escape. On the floor was a crossbow that she had used to fire a rope. The arrow was stuck in a wooden sign on an office building across the road from the mansion, and the thief was balancing her way to freedom.

'She's already three-quarters of the way across!' yelled Ben in frustration.

'No way,' moaned Ollie. 'The diamonds are escaping!'

'No they're not,' woofed Spud. 'If she can do it, then so can I.' The brave puppy looked around for something to help him balance. He grabbed an umbrella from the wardrobe and jumped on to the window sill.

'Don't be daft, Spud,' said Ben. 'Dogs can't walk on a tightrope.'

Normal dogs can't, he agreed. *But maybe spy pups can. I have an idea.* 'Star,' he woofed, take off your collar and clip it to the rope. His sister looked puzzled, but with Sophie's help, did as she was told. 'Now grab one of Lord Partington's ties from the wardrobe and tie it on to my collar . . . and tie the other end to your collar.'

Star dashed over to the closet, nosed it open and jumped up to pull a tie off the rack with her teeth. Sophie worked out what was going on and quickly tied both ends. 'Be quick,' Spud woofed, 'we haven't got much time.'

Sophie understood perfectly. 'So it's like a safety harness,' she beamed. If you fall, the tie is attached to the tightrope so you'll be caught by your collar. Great idea, Spud. What a clever puppy.'

Spud gave her a doggie smile. It was usually his sister who did the clever stuff. *Mmm, not 'great' exactly*, thought the puppy. *But it reduces the risk*.

He stood on his hind legs and took the umbrella in his paws. *This should help with balance*, he thought hopefully, as he took his first step out of the window.

'Careful, bro,' yapped Star. 'You're a doggie, not a squirrel.'

Sophie peeped out from behind her fingers as Spud took his first few tentative steps along the rope. The tightrope lady was way ahead. She had her arms stretched wide, balancing, a professional with twenty years' experience. Spud edged along, his legs wobbling, the closed umbrella keeping him steady.

'Don't look down,' shouted Ollie.

Spud couldn't resist and took a quick glance at the world below. *Yikes!,* he thought. *Good advice, Ollie! Four storeys is very high*. He was above the garden. Next he'd be out of the manor grounds and across the main road. He fixed his eyes ahead and shuffled forward. *Keep going. Just stay calm and follow the lady*. The puppy's paw felt for its next step and he inched along the rope.

The lady had reached the other end of the tightrope. Spud watched as she leapt across to the ledge behind the sign. She reappeared behind the sign and glared across at the puppies and the children. Spud wobbled forward, getting closer to the diamonds. He was halfway. He was taking Ollie's advice, but could hear traffic below. Then his worst nightmare came true.

'You sure are a talented dog,' yelled the tightrope lady. 'I knew you could juggle, but I've never seen a puppy on a tightrope before.'

Thanks, thought Spud. *Now if you can just keep talking while I catch you up.*

'But this is your final act,' laughed the lady as she grabbed hold of the rope. The children watched as she deliberately wobbled it from side to side, then up and down, sending a wave towards Spud. It reached the puppy and he had no chance. First he wobbled and the umbrella swung wildly as he struggled to keep his balance. Then he fell. Sophie's face disappeared behind her hands once more as Spud's safety device kicked into action and he was left dangling by his collar. But instead of death by falling it now seemed like death by strangulation.

The children could hear Spud choking as his body swayed high above the road. His legs kicked, but it was no use, he'd never get back on the rope.

The children looked at each other, eyes tingling with tears. 'Maybe we can catch him!' suggested Ben, and the three children stampeded down the stairs.

Spud's eyes were bulging and his breath was getting short. *Not good*, he winced. His neck was stretched. He could see stars, but he wasn't sure if they were real or just due to lack of oxygen. *A plan*, he thought. *I guess there's only one thing I*

can do. Spud fumbled his paws over the umbrella, feeling for the release button. *Got it*. He pressed the button and the umbrella sprang into bloom. He wriggled hard, trying to free himself from his collar. He felt it loosen a little, but his breath was getting short. He thought his head would explode. *More stars than ever!* Spud dangled dangerously above the road like a fish on a hook. *Another wriggle*. With a final kick of his back legs he finally felt himself slip out of his collar.

The puppy fell to earth like Mary Poppins wafting down on the breeze. The umbrella slowed his fall, but he still landed heavily. Spud looked up and saw headlights coming right at him. The horn blared.

It's too late to escape! Spud crouched low as the lorry passed over him. He leapt to his left to avoid a car and scrambled to the safety of the pavement. *Phew!* By the time the panting children arrived at the road, Spud was dusting himself off and tidying away the umbrella.

'Spud!' woofed his sister, throwing herself at him and knocking him off his feet again. 'I thought you were a goner. You're so brave to have followed that evil woman.'

Spud nodded. 'I guess it was kind of . . .

heroic,' he woofed, proud of his bravery. 'And that landing was pretty cool.'

'The lady got away,' moaned Ollie. 'We need to catch her.'

But Star was already leading the way, bounding towards the circus. There was a baddie on the loose and it was her turn to be a hero!

13. A Safe Place

Lara and the professor stood outside the big top. The show continued inside, but clearly something was wrong. The ringmaster had introduced the rubber man, but he was nowhere to be seen. It was the same story with Gordon Gibbons – the show was monkeyless. The tightrope team had performed with one of their troupe missing and 'The Precious Puppies' had gone walkies. So the clowns had done an extra turn, their rickety fire engine creating more fun for the children.

'So where are the children, GM451?' quizzed the professor, looking all around. 'You indicated they were outside.'

This is where I left them, shrugged Lara. *Surely they didn't follow the pups to the manor?*

From out of the gloom they saw someone

running. And yapping just behind were Star and Spud. 'Get her, Ma,' barked Star. 'She's the baddie. She's got the diamonds.'

Lara didn't need telling twice. GM451 was retired from active service, but she was being handed a criminal on a plate. The lady was exhausted, so very easy to catch. Lara stood on her hind legs and adopted her karate stance.

'Hand over the goodies, lady,' she growled. 'Or I'll have to take you down.'

The woman had already encountered juggling and tightrope-walking puppies, so a

fully grown black-belt dog was the final straw. She gave up without a fight, falling to the grass with sobs of frustration.

'Horrible dogs,' she yelled, 'and awful children.' She beat the grass in frustration. 'They're dangerous!'

'No way,' panted Spud. 'We're only dangerous if you're a baddie. Or a jewel thief. Like you.'

Ben arrived next, his lungs bursting from the chase. 'Ask her, Professor,' he began, hands on hips. 'Ask her to empty her pockets.'

Professor Cortex searched the lady and pulled out a small velvet bag. He untied the ribbon and whistled softly. 'Sparklers,' he gasped, his eyes lit up by the diamonds. 'Probably Lord and Lady Whatsits' diamonds, if I'm not mistaken.'

'Too right,' panted Ben. 'We saw the whole thing, Professor. Spud nearly died in the chase.'

Spud puffed out his chest in pride. 'It was certainly a near-death experience,' he sniffed. 'But all in a day's work for a dedicated spy pup. No need for a medal. But how about some of Mum's home-made chilli?'

Lara glared at her son and his chest reduced. 'You were supposed to observe,' she growled. 'Not chase! Consider yourself grounded.'

'But, Mum,' began Spud. 'That's so unf–'

'And you, lady,' snarled Lara. Star's tail wilted. 'Whatever do you think you two were doing getting yourselves and the children into danger?'

'Sorry, Ma,' whined Star. 'We were only –'

'You were only risking your lives,' barked Lara angrily. 'Spying is all well and good, but you always have to think of safety first.'

Mrs Jewell heard the commotion and came out of the big top. 'What on earth's going on?' she exclaimed. 'What's all the barking? And what's Lucy doing with her face in the mud?'

'Thank goodness you're here,' began Sophie. 'Did you know that your circus is riddled with bad guys? Your husband's not only the ringmaster, he's the ringleader! They've been stealing diamonds and rubies and we've just caught them red-handed. Lucy, your tightrope walker, is one of them. And Gordon Gibbons and the rubber man will wake up in handcuffs.'

Mrs Jewell looked shocked. 'Baddies?' she said, 'In the circus? Including Tony? Surely not.'

'Seems so, Mrs Jewell,' agreed the professor. 'We caught your tightrope walker with these.'

Mrs Jewell's face fell in surprise as the professor opened his hand and showed her a dozen perfect diamonds. 'Probably worth millions,' he said. 'And the gang has been operating for months so they've probably

amassed hundreds of millions by now. The question is,' said the professor, scratching his bald head, 'where have they stashed the rest? We'll need to find your husband to get the answer to that.'

Mrs Jewell puffed out her cheeks. 'Well,' she said, 'I suppose I'd better take them for safekeeping. I'll lock the gems in the safe in my caravan until the police arrive.' There seemed to be relief in her eyes. 'To be honest,' she said, 'it'll be a blessing to be rid of Tony. He's so horrible. Nobody likes him. Will you keep Lucy under your watchful eye, please, and one of you call the police?' Mrs Jewell took the bag and marched to her caravan.

The professor pressed 999 into his mobile. 'All in a day's work,' he smiled as he waited for the call to get through.

'Tell them there are two baddies at the mansion as well,' added Ollie. 'They might need to send an ambulance for them.'

'Err, police, please,' said Professor Cortex. 'At Tony Jewell's circus. I want to report a diamond robbery and to tell you that a couple of spy pups have saved the day!'

14. The Mane Event

As Mrs Jewell strutted back to her caravan, she was cursing under her breath. 'Dratted children,' she muttered. 'And blasted puppies. If I get my way they'll be puppy burgers!' She opened a cupboard and took out a chest. She lowered it to the ground and fiddled with the combination lock. The lid opened and she pulled out some dazzling costumes.

My stupid husband got us into this mess, she thought. *And now it's time for me to make my escape while he pays the price.*

Because her husband wasn't actually involved in the burglaries, he never knew exactly how many jewels came back to the circus, and the thieves never saw the final part of the deal. Tony had entrusted the exchange of goods between himself and the criminals to his wife. But

Jennifer Jewell had been careful never to give him as many as he needed, in the hope that Clarissa White would finally feed him to her fishes. The rest of the precious stones she sewed into the performers' outfits.

I hate caravans, she thought. *This will allow me to escape the circus forever for the life of luxury I deserve!*

It was the perfect crime. Even when the police had searched her caravan they'd only found what they expected – dazzling outfits. They'd assumed the sparklers were worthless cut glass or buttons from the market. But the performers had looked like a million dollars because their outfits had literally been *worth* a million dollars!

She chuckled to herself. 'It was all going so well. All these lovely jewels,' she said, holding a garment up to the light. 'Until tonight! These puppies have ruined everything,' she cursed. Jennifer Jewell stuffed the costumes back into the chest and locked it. She checked the coast was clear and made her way across the car park, struggling under the weight of the treasure chest. The show was coming to an end. Soon the grounds would be teeming with people, but by then she planned to be far away.

'Just to be sure of a distraction,' she purred, 'I'll unlock this door.' Mrs Jewell put the chest down and took out a huge bunch of keys. She fumbled for the right one before carefully inserting it into the lock and turning it with a satisfying *click*. She left the door ajar and scurried away. Mrs Jewell hauled the chest behind her as she looked round for a getaway vehicle. She had to escape before the car park was swarming with customers.

'No time to waste,' she murmured to herself.

All the performers' cars were locked. The only one with keys in was the clown car. 'It's not the fastest,' she muttered, 'but it will at least get me to the nearest station.'

She heaved the costume chest into the back seat and jumped into the vehicle. The engine chugged into life. Mrs Jewell flicked on the lights and the comedy car spluttered out of the car park towards the open road. Jennifer Jewell and the million-dollar outfits had escaped.

So had the lion. It was rare that anyone ever came close to his cage. Angry at being locked up for so long, he'd scratched a few people in his time, and the keeper had erected huge *Danger* signs. He'd been asleep at first, but was woken as the cage door rattled. And then there was the *click* that signified his cage was open. He stretched and yawned. He'd done his part of the show, but this seemed very interesting. The lion nosed at the cage door. It was open. The big cat felt pleased to be out.

Inside the big top the show was coming to an end. There had been a few glitches, but Tony Jewell had covered them up like the true professional he was. Behind the scenes, the clowns were moaning like mad.

'We've had to be on *four* times,' grumbled one of them. 'Covering for that useless rubber man. Where on earth has he got to?'

Lord and Lady Partington had thoroughly enjoyed the show. They'd roared with laughter at the clowns and bitten their nails as the trapeze artists swung in the rafters. The band was playing one last time and the performers were bounding into the circle for a final bow.

'Sounds like it's nearly finished in there,' noted Sergeant Graham.

'Lord and Lady Partington will be delighted with the work you kids have put in. Probably be a reward in it, I should imagine,' nodded one of the officers who had just arrived.

No reward necessary, thank you, thought Star, stretching her neck with pride. *Although one of those diamonds on my collar would look pretty cool!*

'Let's go and get the diamonds from Mrs Jewell,' suggested one of the policemen. The gang strolled over to the ringmaster's caravan and knocked loudly . . . then again, even more loudly. The professor turned the handle and went in. 'Hello,' they heard him call. 'Mrs Jewell, are you in?'

He came out with a puzzled look.

'You won't find her in there,' shouted the tightrope walker, who was sitting handcuffed to a lorry. 'She's the one. Don't you see? She's the brains behind it all. Her husband's a loser. He borrowed too much money and we've had to steal gems to pay it all back.'

The children looked at the professor. He looked blankly back.

'She'll be long gone by now,' smirked the captured villain. 'And the gems with her. You were so close,' she laughed. 'And yet so very very far.'

'That's a bit of a worry,' began one of the police officers.

'Not such a worry as *that*,' woofed Spud, his eyes widening in horror. 'Guys,' he yelped, panic rising in his bark, 'there's a very big pussy cat coming our way!'

Lara shook her head in disbelief. She watched as the lion prowled across the grass. It sat some distance away and licked its lips.

OK, everyone, thought Lara. *We've got some jewels to find, but there's a more pressing concern.*

That-a-way, she whined, jabbing her paw towards the lion.

The policeman dropped his pencil. 'It's a l-l-l–'

'*Lion!*' shouted Ollie. 'A great big massive hungry man-eating lion!'

Thanks, Ollie, thought Lara. '*Man-eating*' – *great for starting a panic!*

'And girl-eating!' squealed Sophie, her bottom lip trembling.

'Let's not panic,' panicked Sergeant Graham, running for the safety of his car.

The lion was glad to be out of his cage, but couldn't really be bothered to eat anyone. At least not until the policeman started running. The lion had been in captivity all its life. It had never actually seen a gazelle, but its instincts were intact. A running man was irresistible. This was as close to a gazelle that it would ever get. So the lion gave chase.

It was much faster than the tubby policeman, who turned to look behind and instantly fell over. The children held their breath as he scrambled back to his feet and galloped towards his car. He yanked the door open a second before the lion pounced. The sergeant jumped in and slammed the door and the lion hit the windscreen with a roar of disappointment. The policeman cowered inside. The lion sat on the car bonnet and stared at the man. It took a nibble at a windscreen wiper.

The sergeant fumbled for his radio. '*PS 945 calling base!*' he yelled. '*Come in, base! Quickly, please. I've got an incident. Over.*'

The radio crackled into life. 'Receiving, 945,' came the radio operator's reply. 'What's the incident?'

'Erm,' the sergeant began. 'I've got an . . . erm . . . thing. It's eating my windscreen wipers. Over.'

There was a moment's silence. 'What sort of *thing*, 945? Over.'

'*A lion*,' blurted the policeman. 'A dirty great man-eating lion. It's attacking me and I need help. Over.'

There was another moment's silence until the lady laughed. 'Nice one, Phil,' she said. 'And I've got a hippo sitting on my knee. You had me there for a minute. Keep up the good work. Over and out.'

15. Bait!

Lara had ushered the children back into the big top. *Their safety is always my number one priority.* Tony Jewell was doing his final thanks and in two minutes a thousand lion meals would be pouring out of the tent. The other policeman was delighted to go indoors. He charged inside to arrest the ringmaster and stop anyone leaving. Lara heard him shout, 'There's no need to panic!' which caused instant panic. She heard squeals and screams from inside the big top.

Lara, Star, Spud and the professor stood bravely, surveying the scene. The lion was sitting on the police car, licking its paws and cleaning its whiskers.

The professor looked at Lara and the spy pups. 'GM451,' he began, 'this is a code red, grade A emergency.'

Obviously, Prof, thought Lara slapping her forehead. *And it's up to us to trap the animal before it actually eats anyone. But how?*

'I've got a plan, Ma,' said Spud, jumping up and down with enthusiasm. 'Lions eat meat, right?'

'Yes.'

'And over there's a hot-dog van, right?'

'Yes.'

'So we need to get some hot dogs and leave a trail back to its cage. Once inside, we lock the door and, hey presto, the big puss is back behind bars.'

Lara considered the plan. 'And the hot dogs would be for the lion, not you, right?'

Spud blushed. 'Of course,' he woofed. 'Most of them, at least!'

'I think it's the best idea we've got,' replied Lara.

'It's the only idea, Mum,' reminded Star. 'And it means someone's got to get into the hot-dog van.'

'What on earth are you mutts barking about?' asked the professor. All doggie eyes fell on the scientist. 'What?' he said. 'Why are you looking at me like that?'

Because you're the bait! thought Spud. *You're the only one who can get into the van.*

The policeman's head poked out from the big top. 'Have you caught it yet?' he hissed. 'These people are getting restless.'

The professor saw the pups looking at the hot-dog van and seemed to understand the plan. 'Not yet,' he replied, 'but I think I'm the bait!' The professor took off his coat. 'I can run quicker without it,' he said, knowing he'd never done a day's exercise in his life. He looked at the lion and then at the fast-food van. 'Here goes.' The professor sidled slowly towards the van. He'd learnt from the policeman's mistake and was taking it step by step. 'Nice pussy,' he soothed. 'Good pusskins.'

The lion gave him a dirty look and a little growl. The professor panicked and set off at a

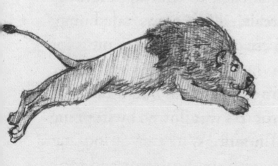

sprint. Once again the lion couldn't resist a chase and bounded after him. The dogs barked. The professor squawked. He wasn't a great runner, but it was amazing what a chasing lion could do. He made it to the van and slammed the door. The lion slowed down and circled, licking its lips.

Inside, Professor Cortex rummaged in some boxes. He found some raw burgers and hot-dog sausages. He threw one out of the window and the big cat took it. *Gulp*. The burger disappeared in one.

'Now we need a temporary distraction,' woofed Star. '*Over here, you big mangy cat!*' The brave puppy ran towards the lion, barking like mad. 'If you want meat, come and try me.'

The lion looked at the dog. And back at the van. The professor was furiously stuffing a bag full of meat. Then back to the yapping dog. Before the lion realized what was happening, the scientist had escaped and was running for the cage, throwing meaty morsels as he sprinted. The lion saw him and bounded off in pursuit, but its progress was slowed by stopping to eat the trail of hot dogs.

Star caught up with the professor and took

the bag in her jaws. 'Out of the way, sir,' she snarled from the side of her mouth. 'I'll take over from here.' The puppy dragged the meaty bag into the lion's cage and waited nervously while the big cat chomped its way home. The lion ventured into the cage and Professor Cortex slammed the door, tying it shut with some rope.

Nice puss, thought Star as she backed away. *Eat your hot dogs. They're much tastier than real dogs!* The lion nosed at the bag of meat and Star took the opportunity of slipping between the bars to safety. *Phew! Being little does have its advantages!*

Professor Cortex sank into a deckchair that was beside the cage in relief. He rummaged in his pocket for his heart pills and rattled some into the palm of his hand. He cupped them to his mouth and relaxed. 'Never been chased by a lion before,' he gasped.

The pups and Lara ran up to him licking him furiously. 'Nice work, Prof,' they yapped.

Sergeant Graham emerged from his car. 'I was about to tackle the lion myself, sir,' lied the cowardly copper. 'But it seems like you've saved me a job. Now, if you don't mind, my colleague and I will send these good people on their way.' He disappeared into the big top to help his fellow officer calm the crowd. A few seconds later, a handcuffed Tony Jewell was led out. He grimaced at the children and dogs as he walked past.

'You lot should have kept your meddling noses out of my circus,' he growled. 'And what good's it done you? Jen's made a clean getaway,' he smirked. He aimed one more kick at the puppies.

But there's no clean getaway for you, thought Spud, dodging the boot.

'I think she must be in our clown car,' added one of the clowns, who had come back from the car park. 'It's gone.'

Tony Jewell laughed. 'She'll be at the train station by now!' he yelled as he was bundled into the back of the police car. 'The diamonds are long gone. "The Precious Puppies" have failed.'

His laugh was cut short as the car door slammed shut. The blue light was switched on and Tony Jewell was driven away.

The group stood gloomily. 'What now?' said Ben. 'This has been an exciting mission, but we've only completed half of it. He's right; Mrs Jewell and the millions have escaped.'

'But she can't have got far if she's gone in the clown car,' piped up Ollie. 'It's got wobbly wheels for a start.'

'So we can give chase,' suggested Ben. 'She might not have made it to the station yet.'

'In what?' snorted Sophie. 'The only vehicles are circus lorries, burger wagons or ice-cream vans.'

Star did a quick calculation in her head. 'Out of those,' she woofed, 'ice-cream vans are fastest. Come on, gang, let's go!'

Star ran to the nearest van and jumped through

the window. *Come on, guys,* she thought. *The driver's still inside the big top. Keys are in. Wagons roll!* She settled into the driver's seat and felt for the key. *Cool!* She used both paws to turn it and the diesel engine rattled into life. Spud had already joined his sister. 'Come on, you guys,' he woofed. 'The gems are getting away!'

16. The Chase

Ben caught on. 'Prof,' he said, 'are you driving or me?'

Professor Cortex shook his head in disbelief. 'You can't drive, Benjamin,' he spluttered. 'You're only twelve and your mother would never forgive me.'

'So you'll have to do it then, Prof,' yelled Ben, grabbing the man's hand and pulling him towards the van. 'And quick, before Mum comes outside!'

Star made room in the front seat. The scientist plonked himself down and familiarized himself with the controls. 'Seems simple enough,' he said. 'Off we go.'

The ice-cream van juddered away. Ben, Sophie and Star sat up front with the professor. Ollie and Spud were in the back, helping

themselves to ice creams. Spud was in doggie heaven. He'd found the flakes and was already on his fourth 99.

Spy pups need to keep their energy up! he thought.

The ice-cream van bounced across the grass and on to the tarmac. The professor hit a few switches, looking for the lights. The road came into view. One of the switches started the ice-cream van tune and off they sped in hot pursuit to the accompaniment of 'How Much is That Doggie in the Window?'.

Meanwhile, Jennifer Jewell was trundling along in the clown car. It was slow and bumpy, but she was making good progress. The station was only another five miles away. She smiled a satisfied smile. Maybe things weren't so bad after all. She'd escaped. She had the jewels. Her idiot husband was going to be locked up for life. The criminal mastermind purred like the lion she'd let out.

It was late at night so there wasn't much traffic. She looked in her rear-view mirror. A van was driving on the road behind her. She frowned and shook her head. She could hear a tune. A faintly familiar tinkling melody. *'How Much is That Doggie?'* she thought. *Sounds like an ice-cream van. That can only mean one thing. One very bad thing.*

The clown car was going as fast as it could. She swung round a tight bend and the ladder on the back came loose. *Drat*, she thought, driving with one hand as she fought to recover the ladder. *This is a ridiculous contraption.*

The ice-cream van was closing on her. She peered in her rear-view mirror again. All the lights in the van were on. She could see several people in the front seat, including a dog. *Not those stupid puppies!*

The professor had his foot to the metal. The

ice-cream van was churning out black smoke and the temperature gauge was rising fast. Everything was rattling, including the professor's false teeth.

'Come on, Prof,' urged Star. 'Nearly caught her.' The professor switched the headlights on to full beam to distract Jennifer Jewell and she was immediately dazzled, nearly swerving off the road. The ice-cream van continued to pump out its tinny music. The playlist was belting out 'Food, Glorious Food' and Spud was humming the tune to himself as he tucked into a choc ice. Ollie had given up.

'I feel sick,' he said, chocolate sauce dribbling down his chin.

The professor gave one last push on the accelerator and rammed the back of the clown car. Mrs Jewell looked over her shoulder in horror. The van was much bigger than her comedy car. She looked at the array of buttons on the dashboard and grinned wickedly. 'James Bond has spy gadgets in his car,' she purred. 'But I'm loaded with clown gadgets.' She flicked the switch marked 'Bubbles' and the ice-cream van was immediately lost in a shiny cloud that burst on the windscreen.

The professor switched on his windscreen wipers and they smeared the oily liquid across the window, obscuring his vision.

'Bad move!' yelled Ben. The ice-cream van left the road and bumped along in a field before Ben helped the professor wrestle the steering wheel back towards the tarmac. They found the window washer button and squirted the windscreen clean.

'Phew,' said the professor, 'that was too close for comfort!' His foot went to the floor again, the engine roaring. 'Follow that clown car!'

Jennifer Jewell wasn't done yet. She flicked the switch marked 'Feathers' and the professor had to navigate through what seemed like a flock of pigeons and then, third time unlucky, he was smoke-bombed. 'This is ridiculous,' he yelled, wiping tears from his eyes. 'We don't have any weapons!'

'We've got ice cream,' shouted Ollie from the back.

'That's a dessert, not a weapon, Oliver,' replied the professor.

'Could be both,' yelled Sophie.

The dogs were yapping and the music was blaring. Professor Cortex changed to a lower gear and prepared to catch up with the getaway car. The engine groaned and the professor's cheeks wobbled as he drew alongside the clown car and waved.

'Pull over!'

The jewel thief glared at the professor. 'Never!' she yelled.

The vehicles were neck and neck. Ollie opened the serving hatch and aimed a spoonful of ice cream at the driver's seat. She took the first scoop on the side of the head. He beamed. 'Want some raspberry ripple, lady?' he yelled, aiming another scoop. 'And I've got toffee fudge.'

The vehicles were tyre to tyre as they rounded

a corner. The clowns' ladder swung towards the van. Without thinking, Star leapt on to the ladder and hung on as it swung back towards the car. 'Careful, girl,' woofed Lara.

Star hung on with her teeth and paws, slowly crawling her way towards the front of the car. Mrs Jewell tried to bat her away. The puppy dodged out of reach and the lady had to look ahead to navigate another bend.

The professor's heart was racing. This was the most exciting chase ever. But just as he was speeding alongside the clown car, on the wrong side of the road, he saw a lorry approaching. Headlights dazzled him. He slammed on the brake and pulled in behind Mrs Jewell's vehicle just as the oncoming lorry careered past, horn blaring.

'Road hog!' yelled the professor, shaking his fist. 'Can't you read the side of my van? It says "Mind that Child!"'

Star was nearly there. Her fur was blowing wildly as she clawed her way towards the baddie. Her ears were flapping. The chest containing the gems was on the passenger seat. *The diamonds must be in there,* she thought.

Mrs Jewell reached out and tried to slap Star

off the ladder again. The puppy jumped to avoid the fist and landed on the treasure chest. The lady jabbed a fist again. *Missed*. And again. *Ouch, that's a hit*. Star was stunned by the blow. The criminal picked the puppy up by the collar and was about to hurl her out of the moving vehicle. Star kicked her legs wildly, wriggling for freedom, but it was no good. Her short life flashed before her. *Certain death!* She looked around frantically. *A big red button on the dashboard*. Star stuck out a paw and hit the 'Eject' button. The lady's face turned white. She dropped the puppy. There was a terrified yowl as she was ejected from the car.

As the car slowed, Star yanked on the handbrake. Professor Cortex hit the brakes at the same time and everyone shot forward. Spud got another face full of ice cream.

Mmm, he thought, licking his chops. *This is the best chase ever*.

The professor, children and dogs jumped from the van. 'Everyone OK?' asked Ben. 'How are you, Star?'

'Good,' wagged the puppy, 'I think. It was my turn to be a hero. How did I do, bro?'

Her brother wagged hard. 'Didn't see too

much,' he admitted. 'I was . . . err . . . busy
with stuff in the back. Missile-launch kind of
stuff. Ollie and I were down to our last lemon
sorbet.'

The crowd gathered under a tree. Jennifer
Jewell was hanging from a branch, legs kicking,
her voice

loud and
shrill. 'I don't
believe this!' she
yelled. 'Defeated
by a pair of good-
for-nothing pups.'

Spud wagged harder than he'd
ever wagged before. 'Good-for-
nothing pups?' he woofed. 'I think she
means "spy
pups".'

17. Fresh Meat

Tony Jewell parked his car in the castle courtyard. He checked himself in the mirror and decided against smoothing his eyebrows. 'No point,' he grumbled. 'They've got a life of their own.'

He stepped out and put his hand to his ear to steady the earpiece. 'Proceed as normal,' said the professor into the microphone. 'We don't want to arouse her suspicions. The puppies have cameras in their collars. If you get us some decent evidence, we can reduce your jail sentence.'

The puppies jumped out of the back seat, wagging enthusiastically. 'Clarissa hates dogs,' hissed the ringmaster.

And we hate baddies, thought Spud. *So that makes us even.*

Tony Jewell rang the bell and the door opened. The dogs trotted in, tails like car aerials. Spud's ears were held high, his bullet hole showing clear daylight.

They were shown through to the white room where the fish tank bubbled with life. Clarissa White's face fell as she saw the dogs. Her cat hissed and jumped from her knee, arching its back as it ran.

'*Remove* those dogs,' ordered Clarissa White. 'You know I can't stand canines!'

'Sorry, Miss White,' said the ringmaster. 'We'll be gone very soon. I've brought the gems. You wanted a million's worth.' He handed over the small velvet bag and watched as the master criminal poured the diamonds into the palm of her hand.

'Excellent, Tony,' she beamed, dropping the jewels back into the bag. 'Your debt is repaid. We're quits.'

'Not quite,' woofed Spud. 'We want those jewels and we want you in prison! Smile for the camera, you're live on Cortex TV!'

Star leapt on to the table and grabbed the tiny bag in her mouth. 'Get away, mutt!' shrieked Clarissa. 'My jewels. Give me my

jewels!' She grabbed at Star, but the puppy escaped. 'They're not your jewels, lady.'

The white cat hissed and bared its claws. It jabbed a paw at Star as she ran by, scratching the puppy's side.

Hope you can see this, Prof, thought Spud. *Cameras are rolling. You have enough evidence. Can we get that dratted cat locked up too? Now let's have some back-up, please!*

Clarissa White's bodyguard was closing in. 'Give me the jewels, doggie,' he growled.

No way, thought Star, flicking her head and tossing the bag out of reach. All eyes followed the velvet pouch as it splashed into the fish tank.

Whoops! Spud watched the bag sink to the bottom of the huge aquarium.

'My diamonds!' screeched the lady. 'Get my diamonds!' She aimed a stare at her bodyguard.

'But, madam,' began the man. 'What about the fish?'

'What about them?' screamed Clarissa White. 'Don't tell me you're afraid of a few little fish. You're supposed to be tough!'

The man remembered the steaks. He looked at his arms and thought about how much meat was in them. 'But, Miss White . . .' he said.

'For goodness' sake, Curtis,' she yelled. 'Give me your jacket.' The burly man took off his jacket and Clarissa White pulled it on, holding the end of the sleeve as she walked to the tank. She grabbed a chair and stood on it. Everyone watched as the lady plunged her arm into the tank and swished it towards the bottom. The fish went into a frenzy, their razor teeth gnashing at the sleeve. Her hand couldn't reach the bottom of the tank, so she leant further over, dangling her whole arm in. Holes appeared in the sleeve and bare skin was exposed. The risk was high, but her greed was stronger.

She leant a bit further, her whole body

dangling over the water, her arm sweeping the tank. Traces of blood started to appear in the water as she clasped the bag. 'Got it!' She tried to back out of the tank, but the chair wobbled and fell away beneath her. She plunged into the water with a muffled shriek and the fish couldn't believe their luck. The jewel thief's face appeared through the glass, eyes wide in horror, hair swirling in slow motion. The fish darted towards her, hungry for their lunch. Tony Jewell looked away.

Spud couldn't bear it. *Think quickly. Think like a spy pup. She's a thief, but nobody deserves to be eaten by piranhas!* He bounded on to the table and picked up a glass paperweight in his mouth. 'Out of the way!' he woofed from the side of his mouth. The puppy hurled the paperweight as hard as he could. It hit the tank and the glass cracked. The pressure of the water did the rest as the aquarium exploded into a thousand pieces and the room was flooded with a tidal wave of water and wriggling fish, their teeth snapping in the fresh air.

The cat was away. He liked a fish supper, but these were just too dangerous to eat. Tony Jewell stood, eyebrows drenched, frozen with

cold water and fear. Clarissa White stood, sodden but triumphant, the black bag clasped in her good hand.

'Oh, no you don't,' woofed Star as she lined up her collar. She pressed the button and the lady felt a pinprick on her neck. Her eyes widened and she took on a confused look. *The professor's truth drug, lady. Confess*, thought Star, pointing the collar camera at the diamond thief.

'You poor fish,' said Miss White, and she started rescuing the flipping piranhas, placing them into a small fish bowl on the sideboard. 'I bought you with stolen money. And I'm such a naughty criminal! Oh, my goodness, all those gems I've stolen! All those people I've threatened. And that time I cheated at Cluedo! Can someone find me a pen and paper so I can write it all down?'

Curtis the bodyguard was off, running for the door. 'My go,' woofed Spud, lining up his collar. The dart hit the man's left buttock, but he kept running. Spud gave chase. They galloped down the stone stairs. 'Another direct hit,' the puppy barked as dart number two found the opposite cheek. The burly man opened the door . . . and there was Professor Cortex.

'Who are you?' demanded the scientist.

The bodyguard looked puzzled. 'Do you know what,' he began, 'I'm not entirely sure.' He pushed past the professor and jumped into Tony Jewell's car. He turned the key and the engine roared into life. Spud and the professor watched as the confused man looked at the dashboard. 'So many buttons,' he said. 'And why have I got three pedals when I've only got two feet?'

Professor Cortex walked over to the car. 'If you'd just come with me, sir, I can explain everything. Believe me, next week, everything will make a lot more sense.'

Spud yapped excitedly. 'Mission accomplished!'

18. Meddling Pups

The family gathered at Partington Manor for the ceremony. Lord Partington smiled at the dogs as he approached the microphone. 'Ahem,' he coughed. 'Thank you all for coming here today.'

No problem, sir, wagged Spud. *Please keep the speech short and let's get to the buffet.*

'We are gathered here today . . .'

Oh crikey, thought Spud, *it's going to be a long one.*

'. . . to thank the Cook family, especially their children. And their wonderful dogs. In particular, the puppies, Spud and Star.'

The crowd broke into warm applause. Lord Partington held up last week's newspaper. 'I'm sure you've all read about the crime and how they solved it?'

More applause. *Come on, man*, sniffed Spud. *I can smell sausage rolls*.

'The police have told us that the circus gang had been operating for a year. They'd amassed several million pounds' worth of gems.'

Lara nodded to herself.

'They were *highly* organized,' the lord continued. 'The parade through town was a means of eyeing up the biggest houses. A monkey would then be sent over the wall to disable the CCTV cameras.'

'Hey,' said Ollie, 'I saw a monkey do that at this house.'

'Exactly,' hissed Sophie. 'Duh!'

'Then it was the same routine every time. Mr Jewell would always give free closing-night tickets to the . . . erm . . . wealthiest families in town, thereby guaranteeing that their homes would be empty on the evening of the final performance. The gang would sneak off and carry out the robbery, arriving back just in time to perform. The perfect alibi. The contortionist would get through the smallest of holes, either a bathroom window or a cat flap.'

'Hey,' said Ollie again, 'I saw him getting through the —'

'*Shush*,' hissed his sister again. 'He's explaining how the pieces all fit together!'

'Next, the alarm would be expertly disabled and the team would get started on the safe. The gang was so well trained that often the owners didn't realize anything was missing until weeks after the circus had left town.'

The dogs puffed out their chests. Star and Spud were proud of their crime-fighting powers and Lara was proud of her puppies.

'But there was more to one of the criminals than met the eye. Mrs Jewell, the costume maker, hid the gems from her husband, sewn into the performers' costumes. Little did the circus staff know that their sparkly outfits were indeed worth millions!' Lord Partington held up one of the puppies' cloaks. 'This small garment alone is worth half a million.'

Phew, thought Star. *I'd have taken better care of it if I'd known!*

'But these fabulous little dogs saved the day,' continued Lord Partington, sweeping his hand towards the proud puppies. 'In fact, they even risked their lives. They walked a tightrope, fought off a lion and took part in a daring car chase.'

Didn't actually fight it off, thought Spud modestly.

And it was an ice-cream van, actually, thought Star, *not a car chase. But I get your point.*

'The remaining gems were supplied to a lady called Clarissa White. Nasty piece of work. Theft, kidnapping, torture . . . she's wanted in just about every country in Europe. The circus had been losing money for some time and they needed a loan. Miss White lent Tony Jewell a huge sum that he could never pay back by legal means, so she devised this get-rich-quick scheme. Clarissa White was the brains behind the whole caper. But I believe that the puppies even saved her from being fish food!'

And we helped save the fish afterwards, wagged Star. *In fact, not a single fish was hurt in the making of this adventure! And all the circus animals have been rescued too. The lion now has all the space in the world, without a hot dog in sight, and the elephant's peanut-eating days are over.*

'Miss White confessed to every crime she's ever committed! Numerous robberies, smugglings, kidnappings and general nastiness. Apparently, she even cheated on her maths GCSE! She can expect a *very* lengthy stay at her Majesty's pleasure.' Lord Partington waited for the applause to die down. 'So, it's with great delight that I ask the Cook children, Professor Maximus Cortex and his secret agent spy dog, GM451, to come up on stage to be presented with their medals.'

Retired secret agent spy dog, sir, corrected Lara as she stood proudly to receive thanks.

The children bounded up, led by Ollie, waving overenthusiastically to the crowd. Lara felt another rush of pride as a medal was placed round her neck. She winked at the puppies. *You next*, she thought.

'But, ladies and gentlemen, please reserve your biggest round of applause for the puppy heroes who risked their lives to thwart the evil criminals. I cannot thank these young dogs enough, not only for recovering my family jewels, but for being such heroes. The so-called "Roving Robbers" are now safely behind bars, apart from the monkeys, who are being safely looked after in a sanctuary with the other animals. So please put your hands together one more time for Spud and Star, our very own Spy Pups!'

Applause, whistles and cheering greeted the

puppies as they bounded onstage. Medals were placed round their necks, after which Professor Cortex presented the pups with an ice cream each. Spud's disappeared in one gulp, but Star was determined to savour the moment. She looked at the crowd. *It's such a proud day.* Flashbulbs made her blink, which helped hide the tears.

Spud noticed his sister's glistening eyes. 'What's up, Star?' he asked.

'It's all too much,' she woofed.

'No problem, I'll help you out,' barked her brother, swallowing his sister's ice cream in one.

'Not the ice cream, silly, the emotion,' she woofed. 'This is the proudest moment of my life. Do you think we'll ever feel this good again?'

Spud considered for a moment. *Solving a major crime, getting a medal and scoffing two ice creams?* 'This is a tough one to beat,' he wagged, 'but I reckon we can give it another go, don't you?

Turn over for a sneak peak of

SPY PUPS
PRISON BREAK

1. Twenty-four Hours

Today . . .

'I'm not sure I want to,' whined Star, her puppy eyes filled with worry. 'It's such a long way down.'

Spud frowned at her. His sister could be so annoying at times. *Here we are, about to do our first parachute jump, and my sis wants to back out!* 'Mum's life depends on us,' he barked gravely. 'She has less than twenty-four hours to live. We are her only chance of survival.'

Star nodded. *He's right*, she thought. *We are spy pups and this time we've got the most important mission of our lives.* She took a deep breath and stepped forward for Professor Cortex to fasten her helmet strap. *Please do it up tightly!*

'Are you spy pups ready?' bellowed the

professor above the roar of the engines. Before the puppies were born the professor had trained their mum to be a spy dog and they knew he was desperate to save her.

Spud wagged hard. 'As I'll ever be,' he nodded.

All eyes fell on Star. She nodded bravely but her body language told another story. She was terrified of heights. She was sure she could tackle just about anything else – sharks, lions, evil villains, enemy spies – but falling from a plane was her ultimate fear. Star and Spud had had a recent adventure that involved sliding down a zip wire and that had made her worse.

'You OK, Agent Star?' asked Professor Cortex. 'You don't have to go through with it.'

Oh yes I do, Prof, she nodded. *This is a life-or-death situation.* Star took a deep breath and saluted the professor. 'Let's do it!'

Professor Cortex reached for the aeroplane door and hauled it open. A gale howled around the cabin, blowing his papers all over the place. 'It's now or never!' he yelled into the wind. 'There's your target.'

Spud bounded to the open door and leant

out into the dark night. Lights twinkled through the wispy clouds below. The puppy followed the professor's finger to a square patch of lights.

Spud breathed the fresh air. 'This is sooooo exciting!' he howled. 'Come on, sis, let's go for it.'

Star edged forward. 'I'm not so sure,' she said. 'It's a long way and it's dark.'

Spud snorted in frustration. 'This is a mission,' he barked. 'And we're in it together.'

He grabbed his sister's collar and hauled her out of the plane. Star disappeared into the night sky with a terrified yowl. Spud saluted the professor. *Best go and catch her up*, he wagged. 'Geronimooooo!' howled the spy puppy as he threw himself into the blackness outside.

The mission had started.

2. *That* Dog!

Three days ago . . .

Mr Big hated queuing. And in prison he had to queue for everything.

It's a good job it's only temporary, he thought as he offered his bowl to the man behind the counter.

His fellow inmate shouldn't really have been on serving duty. He had a streaming cold and Mr Big winced as he did a massive sneeze, sending a snot bomb into the saucepan. He blew his nose into his apron and continued serving. Some green slop was ladled into Mr Big's bowl.

'What's that supposed to be?' he grunted.

'Er, soup of the day,' replied the server, wiping his nose on the back of his hand.

'Which day?' asked Mr Big. 'It looks like something the dog's sicked up.'

'Probably is,' chuckled the man, filling the next inmate's bowl.

Mr Big knew there was no point in arguing. This wasn't any old prison. This was the world's most secure prison. It housed all the worst criminals on the planet and he was proud to be part of it. 'Normal criminals go to wishy-washy prisons,' he told his fellow inmates. 'It's an honour to be in this one. It means we're the real deal.'

Mr Big took a piece of stale bread from the basket at the end of the line and made his way to his usual table. 'Archie, Gus,' he nodded, 'how's the *soup de jour*?'

'Soup de what?' grunted Gus.

'It's French, stupid,' piped up Archie. 'The soup of the day is fantastic,' he smiled. 'And we won't be having too much more of it, will we, boss?' he beamed. 'Not if our plan comes off.'

'"When" not "if",' corrected Mr Big, picking up his spoon and grimacing. The server's sneeze globule was floating in the green goo. He was used to the finer things in life. His criminal mind had brought him wealth beyond the imaginations of most people. He'd owned

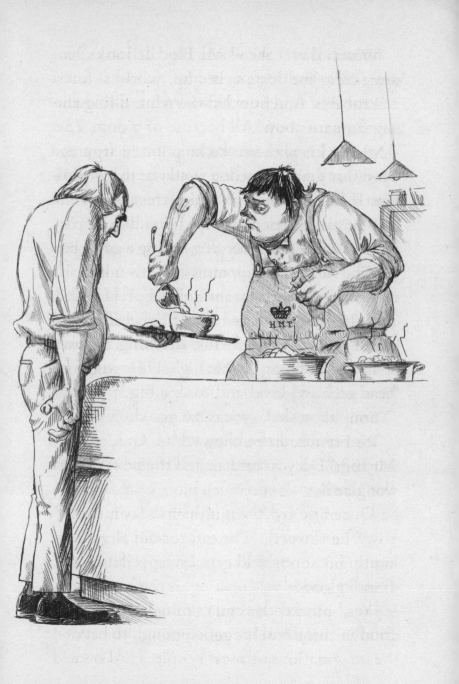

homes all over the world. He'd driven expensive cars and eaten in the world's finest restaurants. And now he was reduced to queuing for snot soup. All because of a dog. *That* dog! But his plan was kicking into action and soon that dratted spy dog would be in big trouble. If his information was correct, she'd had puppies and settled into the good life. Mr Big wasn't interested in the dog having a good life. Having *no life* was uppermost in his mind.

'Are we clear about the next step?' he asked, pushing his untouched soup to one side.

'Yes, boss,' replied Gus, finishing his own soup and reaching for Mr Big's. He lowered his head to bowl level and took a big spoonful. 'Yum,' he smiled, 'yours has got chewy bits.'

'Never mind the chewy bits, Gus,' sighed Mr Big. 'Do you understand the next step of the plan?'

'Our mole says the mutt's birthday is tomorrow,' he slurped. 'The gift should already be waiting. I hope she likes it. I wrapped it myself. It looks good.'

'Yes,' purred the evil criminal. 'Unlike the food in this joint, it's good enough to eat!'

Psssssssssssst!

If you love Puffin Books you should choose

Puffin Post

Est. 2008

Here's what's in it for you:

⭐ **6 magazines**

⭐ **6 free books a year (of your choice)**

⭐ **The chance to see YOUR writing in print**

PLUS

⭐ **Exclusive author features**

⭐ **Articles**

⭐ **Quizzes**

⭐ **Competitions and games**

And that's not all.

You get **PRESENTS** too.

Simply subscribe here to become a member
puffinpost.co.uk
and wait for your copy to decorate your doorstep.

(WARNING – reading *Puffin Post* may make you late for school.)

It all started with a Scarecrow.

Puffin is seventy years old.
Sounds ancient, doesn't it? But Puffin has never been
so lively. We're always on the lookout for the next big
idea, which is how it began all those years ago.

Penguin Books was a big idea from the mind of
a man called Allen Lane, who in 1935 invented
the quality paperback and changed the world.
**And from great Penguins, great Puffins grew,
changing the face of children's books forever.**

The first four Puffin Picture Books were hatched in 1940 and the
first Puffin story book featured a man with broomstick arms called
Worzel Gummidge. In 1967 Kaye Webb, Puffin Editor, started the
Puffin Club, promising to **'make children into readers'**.
She kept that promise and over 200,000 children became
devoted Puffineers through their quarterly instalments of
Puffin Post, which is now back for a new generation.

Many years from now, we hope you'll look back and
remember Puffin with a smile. **No matter what your age
or what you're into, there's a Puffin for everyone.**
The possibilities are endless, but one thing is for sure:
whether it's a picture book or a paperback, a sticker book
or a hardback, **if it's got that little Puffin
on it – it's bound to be good.**